石雕与蝴蝶 —— 胡弦诗选

（汉英双语）

胡弦 / 著
谢炯 / 译

Stone Sculpture and Butterfly
The Selected Poems of Hu Xian

(Chinese – English Edition)

中国青年出版社

胡弦

1966年出生于江苏徐州,现居南京,为《扬子江诗刊》主编,诗人、散文家,出版诗集《阵雨》(2015)、《十年灯》(2015)、《沙漏》(2016)、《不归家的人》(2016)、《空楼梯》(2017)。曾多次获全国大奖,如《诗刊》"新世纪十佳青年诗人"称号(2009)、第三届闻一多诗歌奖(2011)、徐志摩诗歌奖(2012)、柔刚诗歌奖(2014)、《诗刊》年度最佳诗人奖(2014)、腾讯书院最佳诗人奖(2016)、花地文学奖年度诗人(2017)、《十月》文学奖(2018)、《星星诗刊》年度诗人奖(2018)、鲁迅文学奖(2018)。他的作品被翻译成英、法、俄、韩等多国文字。

Hu Xian

Poet, essayist, and editor-in-chief of *The Yangtze River Poetry Journal,* Hu Xian was born in Xuzhou, Jiangsu province in 1966. His poetry and essay collections include *Rain* (2015), *Ten Year Lamp* (2015), *Hourglass* (2016), *The One Who Never Returned* (2016), and *Empty Staircases* (2017). His awards include *Poetry Periodical* "New Century Ten Best Young Poets" (2009), Wen Yiduo Poetry Award (2011), Xu Zhimuo Poetry Award (2012), Rougang Poetry Award (2014), *Poetry Periodical* "Best Poetry of the Year (2014), Tengxun Academy Literature Award (2016), Huadi Literature Poet of the Year (2017), October Literary Award (2018), *Xingxing Poetry Journal* "Poet of the Year" Award (2018), and Lu Xun Literature Award (2018). His works had been translated into English, Korean, Russian, French, etc.

谢炯

诗人，律师，诗歌翻译家，出生于上海。八十年代就读于上海交通大学工业管理系，1988年留学美国，取得企业管理硕士和法律博士学位。2000年在纽约创办自己的律师事务所，为美国知名移民法律师和双语作家。出版有个人诗集《半世纪的旅途》（2015）、散文集《蓦然回首》（2016）、诗集《幸福是，突然找回这样一些东西》（2018）、翻译集《十三片叶子：中国当代优秀诗人选集》（2018）、随笔微小说集《随风而行》（2019）、诗集《黑色赋》（2019）、翻译集《保罗·奥斯特诗歌全集》（2019）。2017年荣获首届德清莫干山国际诗歌节银奖。作品在海内外各文学杂志广为发表，并入选海内外多种选本。

Joan Xie

Poet, lawyer, poetry translator. Born in Shanghai, Xie studied industrial administration in Shanghai Jiaotong University in 1980s. She came to the United States in 1988 to study business and law. In 2000, after receiving an MBA and J.D., she established her law practice in New York City. A well-known immigration attorney today, Xie is a prolific writer in both English and Chinese. Her books include *Half-Century Journey* (2015, poetry), Looking Back (2016, prose), *Nothing Made Me Happier than Finding These Objects* (2018, poetry), *Thirteen Leaves: Selected Poems of Contemporary Chinese Poets* (2018, translation), *Walk with the Wind* (2019, prose), *Song of Blackness* (2019, poetry), *The Collected Poems of Paul Auster* (2019, translation). An award winner at the 2017 First Moganshan International Poetry Festival in China, Xie's works have been selected into several analogies and published widely in both countries.

目录	Catalogue
左手	Left Hand / 002
花园	Garden / 004
观城隍庙壁画	Mural Paintings at City God Temple / 006
花事	Flower-thing / 008
年轻的时辰	Young Days / 010
雪	Snow / 012
琥珀里的昆虫	Insect in Amber / 014
蚂蚁	Ant / 016
树	Tree / 020
夹在书里的一片树叶	A Leaf Pressed in a Book / 022
裂隙	The Crack / 028
镜子	Mirror / 030
影子	Shadow / 032
钟表之歌	Song of a Timepiece / 036

绳结	A Knot in the Rope / 040
蝴蝶	Butterfly / 042
在下雨	Raining / 044
风	Wind / 046
印刷术	Printing / 050
卵石	Pebble / 052
梦	Dream / 054
见鬼	Seeing a Ghost / 058
光	Light / 060
老手表	A Vintage Wristwatch / 062
鸟在叫	The Bird is Chirping / 064
灯	Lamp / 066
树林	Forest / 070
墙	The Wall / 072

老街	Old Street / 074
老火车	Old Train / 076
陪父亲住院	Staying with My Father at the Hospital / 080
初春	Early Spring / 084
窗	Window / 086
石雕	Stone Sculpture / 088
悬浮	Suspension / 090
涌泉	Artesian Spring / 092
讲古的人	Storyteller / 094
剧情	Plot / 098
后主	Last Emperor / 102
北风	North Wind / 104
地图鱼	Map Fish / 106
雅鲁藏布江	Yaruzangbu River / 108

仙居观竹	Viewing Bamboo at the Immortal's Abode / 110
嘉峪关外	Outside Jayu Pass / 112
春风斩	Spring Wind Beheading / 114
星	Star / 116
闻笛	Listening to a Flute / 118
采药人	Herb Picker / 120
沙漠	Desert / 122
篝火	Bonfire / 124
源头	The Source / 126
平武读山记	Reading the Mountains in Pingwu / 128
星相	The Movement of Stars / 130
水龙头	Faucet / 134
玛曲	Maqu / 136
猫	Cat / 138

风中的事	Things in the Wind / 142
窗前	At the Window / 144
在南京	In Nanjing / 146
航班晚点	Flight Delayed / 148
某园，闻古乐	In a Garden, Listening to Ancient Music / 150
邻居	My Neighbor / 152
明月	Bright Moon / 156
姜里村	Jiangli Village / 158
鱼化石	Fish Fossil / 160
蟋蟀	Cricket / 162
卵石记	Notes of a Pebble / 168
面具	Mask / 172
明月	Moon / 176
弹奏	Playing Music / 180

宣纸	Rice Paper / 182
雨	Rain / 184
咖啡馆：忆旧	In a Coffee Shop: Recalling the Past / 186
阅读	Reading / 188
蜡烛	Candle / 190
峡谷记	Canyon / 192
蛇	Snake / 196
倾听	Listening / 200
初春	Early Spring Day / 202
天文学	Astronomy / 204
果园	Orchard / 208
当归	Angelica / 210
初秋书	The Book of Early Autumn / 212
深夜的十字路口	Late Night at the Crossroad / 214

蝶	BUTTERFLY / 216
夏花	Summer Flower / 218
私生子	Illegitimate Child / 220
登天	Up to The Sky / 222
传说	Legend / 226
称体重	Weighing Myself / 228
箭毒蛙	Piercing a Poisonous Frog / 230
致谢词	Acknowledgement / 232

左手

右手有力。
左手有年久失修的安宁。

总是右手相握,在我们中间
打一个死结;或者

像个有力的扳道工。当生活
这列火车从右侧呼啸而过。左手,
在左侧有了另外的主张。

右手前伸,
左手还滞留在记忆中。
 "某些间隙,世界就像消失了……"
无所事事时,右手
会不经意间握住左手,
像握着一件纪念品。

Left Hand

The right hand is dominant.
The left hand exists in dilapidated peace.

Always the right hands clasp, tight a dead knot,
or shunt between us like a powerful

switchman. When the life-train
whizzes passing from the right, the left hand
starts to have other ideas.

Right hand extends forward
while the left stays in memory.
"In some gaps, the world is disappearing..."
When there's nothing to do, the right
will unknowingly grasp the left,
like holding a souvenir.

花园

你知道当我坐在这条长凳上时
许多年代已过去了,
许多人许多事,有的消失,有的
已被写进了书里。

当我坐在这条长凳上,
当不知名的鸟儿鸣叫,
当不识字的南风一次次经过,我意识到为此
写一首诗的确是多余的。

地上,斑驳的树影和从前一样,
除了那向每阵风倾斜的新枝。
无数被混淆的岁月,沙沙响。
一座花园,正是那失而复得的花园。

Garden

You know, as I sit down on this bench
many eras have gone by,
many people and many things, some vanished,
others were written into a book.

As I sit down on this bench,
a nameless bird chirping,
and wordless south wind blowing, again and again,
as if to tell me that poetry is indeed a luxury.

On the ground, the tree's mottled shadow
is as before, except a new twig tilts to each gust of wind.
Countless jumbled days make rustling sounds,
Here in a garden — a lost garden regained.

观城隍庙壁画

壁画中,死者们在裸体接受审判。所以,
从明天起,我准备练一练腹肌,最起码
要把小肚腩练下去,以免到时候
脱了衣服太难看。
我还注意到,并不是所有受审者
都束手就缚,他们在拼命反抗,挣扎。所以
从明天起,我打算天不亮就去长跑,不能
让那些人在美梦中睡得太踏实。
形势逼人呀,我还要多去健身房,因为
即便死后,有一把子好力气也如此重要。

Mural Paintings at City God Temple

In murals, the dead are put on trial naked.
So, starting tomorrow, I intend to exercise
my abdominal muscles, at least to flatten my belly
to avoid shame when it's my turn on trial.
I also noticed that not all the dead obeyed orders;
some struggled and fought hard. So,
starting tomorrow, I intend to run a marathon
before daybreak. I can't let those others sleep in peace.
Things are getting drastic! I must also go to the gym
for it's crucial to have strong muscles
even after my death.

花事

江水像一个苦行者。
而梅树上,一根湿润的枝条,
钟情于你臂弯勾划的阴影。

灰色山峦是更早的时辰。
花朵醒来。石兽的脖子仿佛
变长了,
伸进春天,索要水。

Flower-thing

River resembles an ascetic.
Yet in the plumtree, a wet twig
yields itself to the shadow cast by your curved arm.

Grayness was hills at an earlier time of day.
Flowers wake up. The neck of a stone beast
seems to get longer,
stretches into springtime, begging for water.

年轻的时辰

楼上有个小孩子在弹钢琴,
反复弹一支简单的曲子。
——部分已熟练,部分尚生疏。
我听着,感觉此刻的生活,
类似这琴声变调后的产物。

我的母亲和伯母在隔壁闲话,
谈论着琐事,和她们敬仰的神。
河水从窗外流过,
那神秘、我不熟悉的控制力,
知道她们内心的秘密。

墙上挂着祖母发黄的照片,
白皙的手,搭在椅子黝黑的扶手上。
她年轻而安详,像在倾听,
也许她能听见,这琴声深处
某种会反复出现的奇迹。

Young Days

Upstairs, a young kid plays piano,
repeating a simple sonata
— familiar with some notes, but not the others.
Listening, I feel that jarring sounds
are setting the tone for this moment of life.

Next door, my mom and aunt are gossiping
about minor issues, and a god whom they both worship.
The river flows by the window, carrying their secrets
in its mysterious current, a controlling force
that I'm not yet familiar with.

On the wall, in a yellowed picture,
my grandmother, white hands on an inky black armrest,
young and serene, as if she were listening too.
She might hear the miracle
recurring in the depths of the sonata.

雪

爱是佯装在画其它事物,
把空白的地方叫做雪。

恨是谈论爱那样谈到恨,谈到
疲惫被理解成沉默,
天地都静了,只剩下雪飞。

无所谓爱与恨是堆雪人,
是把一个不相干的人领来尘世,
并倾听
它内心的雪崩。

Snow

Love is to pretend to draw something else
but to call the space left empty — snow.

Hate is to talk of hatred just as you would talk of love
until fatigue is mistaken for silence.
The world is quieting down, only snow whirls.

Indifference is to make a snowman,
to bring an irrelevant being to this world,
while listening to
the avalanche inside of him.

琥珀里的昆虫

它懂得了观察,以其之后的岁月。
当初的慌乱、恐惧,一种慢慢凝固的东西吸走了它们,
甚至吸走了它的死,使它看上去栩栩如生。
"你几乎是活的," 它对自己说,"除了
不能动,不能一点点老去,一切都和从前一样"。
它奇怪自己仍有新的想法,并谨慎地
把这些想法放在心底以免被吸走因为
它身体周围那绝对的平静不能
存放任何想法。
光把它的影子投到外面的世界如同投放某种欲望。
它的复眼知道无数欲望比如
总有一把梯子被放到它不能动的脚爪下。
那梯子明亮、几乎不可见,缓缓移动并把这
漫长的静止理解为一个瞬间。

Insect in Amber

He knows how to see now, including his own fate.
The slow solidification took away his initial anxiety
   and fear,
even his death. He looks alive now.
"You're almost alive", he tells himself, except
"you can't move or grow old; you are just the same
   as before."
He is surprised that he still has new ideas.
Unable to store them in the absolute stillness around him,
he holds them at the bottom of his heart, so they won't
   be sucked away.
The light casts his shadow like a desire into the
   outside world,
his compound eyes see countless desires, for instance:
below his immovable feet, there is always a ladder,
bright, barely invisible, shifting slowly
and mistaking his long stillness for a brief moment.

蚂蚁

蚂蚁并不惊慌,只是匆忙。
当它匆匆前行,没人知道它想要什么,尤其是
当它拖动一块比它的身体
大出许多倍的食物时,你会觉察到
贪婪里,某种辛酸而顽固的东西。
有时成群结队的蚂蚁会形成
一条黑色小溪,纤细脚爪
拖动光阴细碎的阴影;而无数
沿着触须消逝的瞬间,是变形的苦楚,如同
它建在墙根的巢穴,同样隐秘,
不被注意,让我拿不准
是什么,正通过那里向黑暗中流去。
雨水沤坏过天花板,巢穴一直安然无恙。
风雨之夜,我读报、倾听,没有蚂蚁的消息。我知道,
我们都爱着自己的沉默,就像爱惜自己的家
那简陋的入口。有次买家具,我把床
拆成几段,好让它从房门安然通过。另一次
是拆迁,础石被撬掉了,我忽然想到蚁穴,但,
所有的蚂蚁都已无影无踪。

Ant

Not panicking, just keeping busy.
No one knows what an ant wants when it hurries ahead
toppling as it drags a piece of food
much more prominent than itself.
You note a poignant stubbornness in its kind of greed.
An army of ants form a black creek, tiny feet
dragging snatches of flickering time, with freakish pangs
In their feelers flushing countless gone moments,
Like their nest at the bottom of the wall, just as hidden
and overlooked, it makes me wonder
what's flowing through there into the darkness?
Rain damaged the ceiling, but the nest is safe.
On a stormy night, I read newspapers, listen carefully
but no news of ants. We all treasure our own silence
like those tiny doors to our houses.
One time, I bought a bed and had to dismantle
to take it through the door.
Another time, a foundation stone was removed during
    demolition.

偶尔，有刺疼从皮肤上传来，我的手
拍过去，一只小蚂蚁已化作灰尘……
——我几乎不再懂得悲伤，但我知道什么是
蚂蚁的忧虑；所以，
看见细小的枯枝，我会想到庙宇中宏大的梁柱。
另外一些情景稍有不同，比如
一只落单的蚂蚁爬上我的餐桌，仿佛在急行中猛然
意识到了什么，停住，于是有了一瞬间的静止。
在那耐人寻味的时刻，世界上
最细小的光线从我们中间穿过：它把
圆鼓鼓的小肚子，
柔软地，搁在我们共同的生活上。

I suddenly thought of the ant
but all the ants had gone.
Occasionally, a stinging pain pricks my skin,
With the flat of my hand, I smash a small ant into dust…
— no longer bothering to grieve, yet I know
what makes an ant tick while a withered twig
reminds me of a giant pillar in a temple.
Other scenes are slightly different: when a lone ant
crawls onto my table and rushes about,
then stops abruptly, stays put awhile,
as if realizing something; in that intriguing moment,
the world's faintest ray of light passes between us:
that is when the ant softly places its belly,
tiny and bulging, on our shared life.

树

树下来过恋人,坐过
陷入回忆的老者。
没人的时候,树冠孤悬,
树干,像遗忘在某个事件中的柱子。
有次做梦,我梦见它的根,
像一群苦修者——他们
在黑暗中呆得太久了,
对我梦中的光亮感兴趣。
——不可能每棵树都是圣贤,我知道
有些树会死于狂笑,另一些
会死于内心的自责声。所以,
有的树选择秘密地活着,把自己
同另外的事物锁在一起;
有的,则在自己的落叶中行走,学会了
如何处理多余的激情。

Tree

Under the tree, lovers came
an old man too, sat lost in memory.
When no one is there, the tree's canopy arcs alone,
the trunk, a pillar forgotten in the course of an event.
One time I dreamed about its roots
like a group of ascetics – too many years in the dark,
they were only interested in my dreamt-of light.
— It's impossible for every tree to become a sage.
Some will die of laughter, and others will die
from blaming themselves. And so,
Some choose to live secretly,
locking themselves together with something else;
And others will walk among their own fallen leaves,
having learned to deal with excessive passion.

夹在书里的一片树叶

愈来愈轻,侧身于错觉般的
黑暗中:它需要书页合拢,以便找到
故事被迫停下来的感觉。
书脊锋利,微妙的力
压入脉络,以此,它从心底把某些
隐秘的声音,运抵身体那线性、不规则的边缘。
"没有黑暗不知道的东西,包括
从内部省察的真实性。"
它愈来愈干燥,某种固执的快感在要求
被赋予形体(类似一个迷宫的衍生品)。
有时,黑暗太多,太放纵,像某人
难以概括的一生……
它并不担心,因为,浩大虽无止息,
唯一的漩涡却正在它心中。它把
细长的柄伸向身体之外
那巨大的空缺:它仍能
触及过去,并干预到早已置身事外的
呼啸和伤痛。"岁月并不平衡,你能为
那逝去的做点什么?"

A Leaf Pressed in a Book

Increasing in lightness, deferring to a darkened illusion:
it needs to be pressed by the pages to sense
that its story has been forced to halt.
Sharp spine, with a subtle force
pressed into its veins, so it delivers
a mysterious sound from its heart's bottom to
its straight yet irregular body edge.
"There's nothing that darkness doesn't know,
including the truth from inner reflection."
Increasing in dryness,
a certain persistent pleasure insists on taking
a form (similar to those derived from a maze).
Sometimes, it's too dark, too indulgent,
just like a hard-to-categorize life ...
but the leaf worries at nothing, for the sole vortex
swirls in its heart, vast without end.
It extends its slim stem to the huge void
outside: it can also touch the past and intervene
in noise and hurts that long since turned aloof.
"The years aren't balanced, what can you

do for those long gone?"

许多东西在周围旋转：悬念、大笑、自认为
真理的某个讲述……偶尔，受到相邻章节的牵带，
一阵气流拂过，但那已不是风，只是
某种寻求栖息的无名之物。
"要到很久以后，你才会知道发生了什么，
以及其中，所有光都难以
开启的秘密。"
有次某人翻书，光芒像一头刺目的
巨兽，突然探身进来，但
失控的激情不会再弄乱什么，借助
猎食者凶猛的嗅觉和喘息，它发现，
与黑暗相比，灼亮
是轻率、短暂的，属于
可以用安静来结束的幻象。
"适用于一生的，必然有悖于某个
偶然的事件……"当书页再次打开，黑暗
与光明再次猝然交汇，它仍是
突兀的，粗糙与光滑的两面仍可以
分别讲述……
——熟谙沉默的本质，像一座

Many things whirl about: suspense, laughter,
self-righteous talk of the truth...
Occasionally, the air blows, affected by the next
chapter, but it's not the wind,
just something nameless wanting to rest.
"Only years later will you know what happened,
and the secrets that not yet penetrated by the light. "
Once, someone opened the book,
and light burst in like a giant glaring beast
but violent passion could no longer disturb the order.
Helped by the sharp senses of a predator, it realized
that the firelight, compared to the darkness
was careless and short,
an illusion ended with silence.
"What is suitable for a lifetime must be different
   from what is suitable for any given occasion..."
When the book is opened again,
the darkness converges with the light again,
still jarringly, so its rough and smooth sides
can still be described differently...
— well-versed in the essence of silence,

纸质博物馆里最后的事,它依赖
所有失败的经验活下来,心中
残存的片段,在连缀生活的片面性,以及
某个存在、却始终无法被讲述的整体。

like the final doings in a paper museum,
it survives, relying on the failures it's undergone;
its remnant episodes are stringing together
life's one-sided aspects, along with a certain totality
that exists, but could never be narrated as a whole.

裂隙

从完整的事物,它开始,
让一颗没有准备的心,
突然有了此岸与彼岸。

于是,有人学习造桥,
有人学习造船……

一个未知的幽灵在掌控这一切,并为远航
培养出了出色的水手。直到

它彻底裂开,
互不相干的两半被一段
空白隔开。

看上去,各自完整;
看上去,裂隙仿佛已不在场。

The Crack

From something whole, it begins,
and separates its unprepared heart
suddenly there are near and far shores.

Then, someone learns to build a bridge,
and someone learns to make a boat...

An unknown soul controls all these, and trains
good sailors for a voyage afar, until

something breaks,
the two unrelated halves are separated
by a blank space.

It looks as if each half were complete
and the crack had never been present.

镜子

镜子从不记忆,
什么都不能使它激动。

它用一生练习放弃,
笑面、华裳、怒目与鬼脸……
溺死者,会重新出现在镜子外面,
在握手或拒绝中
转过身来。

镜子,总是站在世界的另一侧,
不起伏,不掌控;
面对那么多悲欢离合,
不忠告,不参与。
当许多人远去,它独自留下,
一个深邃、寂静的空间,
等着接下来走向它的人。

Mirror

Mirror memorizes nothing,
nothing can excite it.

All its life, it studies how to give up,
a smiling face, beautiful clothes, glares, and grimace...
the drowned ones will reappear outside the mirror,
amid handshakes or rejection,
turning this way.

Mirror, always stands on the other side of the world,
having no ups and downs, exerting no control;
Facing so many joys and sorrows,
it gives no advice, nor will it join in.
When many people walk away, it alone stays,
in a vast, silent space, waiting
for the next one approaching.

影子

——沉默而平静。间或,
用猛烈的摇晃
表达不属于它的焦灼。

当你沉思,它谦逊地
陪着你沉思。
有时,则拉长又拉长,像你留在
生活中的把柄。
但从没有谁能抓住它。
当你起身,它也立即
从复杂的现场抽身离去。

随时变形,并用变形
保留一种很难被理解的真实。
追逐光对你的
每一种叙述;触摸世界以其
万物难以觉察的手,

Shadow

— Still and calm, or occasionally
shakes violently, expressing
an anxiety not its own.

When you are deep in thought,
it accompanies you humbly.
Sometimes, it stretches, longer and longer,
like dirty laundry you left behind in this world
that no one can catch.
When you get up, it also disentangles itself
right away from a complicated setting.

It shapeshifts at any time to preserve
the hard to comprehend truth;
it chases each story
that the light tells about you; it touches the world
with its hand hardly discernible by living things.

不被注意,但从未离开,只是你
并不知道这意味着什么。

偶尔,会用突然的站立在墙壁上
迎面出现,
吓你一跳。而当你朝它问询或吼叫,
它却认为:
有声音的事物都是荒谬的。

No one paid attention to it, but it never left. And you
don't know what this means.

Occasionally, it will suddenly appear ahead,
standing on a wall
to scare you. But when you question it or bark at it,
it thinks:
all the sound-making things are ridiculous.

钟表之歌

我不替谁代言。
我这样旋转只是想表明
我无须制造漩涡也是中心。
在我这里没有拖后出现的人,也不存在
比原计划提前发生的事。
一切都在我指定的某个时刻上。
我在此亦在彼,在青铜中亦在
镜像中。当初,
是我从矿石中提炼出铁砂,
是我让大海蔚蓝山脉高耸,
是我折磨月亮让它一次次悔过自新,因为
这也是真理产生的方式。
所有的上帝和神都从我这里出发
又回到我这里。
我建立过无数已毁灭的国家今后仍当如是。
除了我的滴答声并不存在别的宗教。
我的上一个念头是北欧的雪崩下一个

Song of a Timepiece

I don't speak for others.
By rotating this way, I simply show
that I am a center, even without creating a vortex.
Here with me, no one's appearance is delayed, nor
 do events
ever happen earlier than initially planned.
Everything is at the moment designated by me.
I am here and there, in bronze
and in the mirror too. In the beginning,
it was I who extracted iron granules from ore,
It was I who blued the sea and towered mountains,
It was I who tortured and forced the moon to mend its ways
again and again, for only thus could the truth be
 squeezed out.
God and gods all start from me
and come back to me.
I've built countless empires, now ruined, with more to come.
There is no other religion except my ticking.
My last thought was a Northern Europe avalanche,
the next one will be a pigeon on a Chinese eave.

会换成中国屋檐上的鸽子。
我让爆炸声等同于咳声,
我让争吵的政客和哭泣的恋人有同一个结局。
我是完美的。不同的语言述说
同样的鸟、城市、天空,这是我的安排。
我创造世界并大于这世界。
我不哭不笑不解释不叹息因为
这永远不是问题的核心。
当我停步我仍能把你们抓牢犹如
国王在宫殿里打盹,远方
军队在消灭它能找到的东西。

I equalize an explosion-sound and a cough,
I give the same ending to quarrelsome politicians and
    weeping lovers.
I am perfect. I arrange different languages to describe
the same birds and city and sky.
I create a world not more than this world.
I don't cry or laugh or explain or sigh
for this is never the core of issues.
When I stop, I can still hold you tight
like a king who naps in the palace
while his army is destroying whatever it can find.

绳结

绳上有个结。绳子
就是在那里找到自己的。

一个死结。任你怎么用力也无法
把它从里面拉出来。

通常,绳子活在一根平滑的线上。
但它内心起了变化,一个结
突然变成身体陌生的部分,被缚住,
并于绷紧中一再被确认。

如同连自身
也不肯放过的仇恨,这用力
拉拽过的结已很难凭回忆解开。
——它认出了思虑无法捕捉的东西,
束紧它,不松开。

A Knot in the Rope

There's a knot in the rope. Rope
finds itself here.

A dead knot. No matter how hard you try,
no way to free it up.

Typically, the rope leads a life of smooth lines
but its heart has changed, a knot
then suddenly becomes a strange body part, tied up
and repeatedly confirmed in its tightness.

As if the hatred must
hate itself, and this forcefully pulled knot
can't be untied by memory.
— it recognizes something uncatchable by thought,
ties it up, and won't let it go.

蝴蝶

颤抖的光线簇拥,蝴蝶
从一个深深的地方
浮向明亮的表面:
—— 一件古老、受罪的遗物,

穿过草丛、藤蔓、痉挛、
非理性……把折痕
一次次抛给空气,使其从茫然中
恢复思考的能力。

翅膀上,繁密的花纹在对抗
制造它的线条,有时
叠起身体,不动,像置身于一阵风
刚刚离去的时间中。

当它重新打开,里面是空的,
没有任何我们想要的东西。

—— 那是一次次重新
飞临的蝴蝶,仿佛
于回声外的虚无中获得过
另外的一生。

Butterfly

Escorted by quivering rays,
from a place of great depth,
the butterfly floats to a bright surface:
— an ancient, beleaguered relic,

passing through grass, vines, convulsion,
again and again… irrationality
extends its creases into the air, to regain
its ability to think in turmoil.

On its wings, a dense pattern is resisting
the lines of its fabrication, sometimes
it folds its body, in stillness, as if in the moment
after a gust of wind has just passed.

When it reopens, empty inside,
there is nothing we want.

— renewed again and again
the butterfly arrives, as if it had lived
another life in the nothingness
beyond all echoes.

在下雨

在下雨。雨
不紧不慢下着,天下无事。
衣服挂在墙上,我们的屋檐滴着水,
没有让雨分心的东西。
在下雨,雨点连成一串,又断掉,
来不及做的事没人做就像
一首诗恰是那不存在的诗。
在下雨,没有停的迹象,像无数雨之前
无法追忆的某场雨:彼时,
天下无事,略同于眼前,人间
无语可论,无偏可执,
只下雨。

Raining

It's raining. Rain
takes its time; nothing happens.
Our clothes hanging on the wall, eaves dripping water,
nothing distracts the rain.
It's raining. Raindrops connect in a line, then break;
not-yet-done things won't be done by anyone, just as
a poem is none other than the non-existent poem.
It's raining, no sign of stopping, the same as that rain
before countless rains, beyond recall: at that time,
nothing happened, the same as now,
the world was wordless, unbiased,
and raining.

风

也许你永远不会知道,
风在怎样经过。

当一个人远去,没有音讯,
只有风声。当一个人
从远方归来,
已变成一段难以把握的感情。

也许你永远不会知道,
风在带走,还是在放下,
穿过某个事件时,它曾怎样
与那中间的火苗相遇。

它吹着岩石,推敲其沉默;
吹着水,吹着患有不孕症的平面。
有时,你以为一切都过去了,
但风在吹,过往的一切
又在风中重来。

Wind

Perhaps you would never know
how the wind passed.

When a man walked away, no message came,
only the wind. When a man
returned from afar,
the feeling between you two became
difficult to handle.

Perhaps you would never know
whether the wind carried the thing away, or let it go,
or when it passed through a thing, how
it met the flame in its core.

It blows over the rocks, honing their silence;
It blows over the water, sweeping its infertile surface.
Sometimes when you believe that everything is passed,
the wind is blowing, all things of the past
are back again in the wind.

有时没有风,寂静
像一种面向虚无的呼吸。
有时,风吹着吹着就散了,
带着根深蒂固的伤感。

有时大风过后,码头和船
像剩在世间之物。
但你仍然不知道,风
是个虚构的秘密,
还是某种无法探究的实体。

Sometimes, there is no wind, the stillness
is like breath drawn in nothingness.
Sometimes, the wind blows, blows away into oblivion
taking with it a deep sadness.

Sometimes after a heavy wind, the pier and boat
are the only things remaining in the world.
But you still don't know whether the wind
is a fictitious secret
or a substance that can't be analyzed.

印刷术

有时是褪色的油漆,
让我看见斑驳的日子
和其中的幸福。

有时是变形的符号
让我同时在几条路上走着。
我经过殿堂,并知道它们是不存在的,
因为另一条路上有它的废墟。

有时我遇见漂浮的梦,
梦中的情人有孤独的肩膀。我不知道
那是离开了谁的胸膛的肩膀。

时间向未来倾倒而去,
但这不是人生失衡的原因。
我遇见烧焦翅膀的鸟,
像一群失眠者。

遇见印错了的字,笔划和结构
是陌生的几何学。
——它锁住的事物鲜为人知。

Printing

Sometimes, a faded shade of paint
let me see the dappled days
and happiness within.

Sometimes, a deformed symbol
let me walk on several paths at once.
I passed a hallowed hall, knowing its non-existence
because of its ruins on another path.

Sometimes I encountered a floating dream
of lovers who had lonesome shoulders. I didn't know
whose shoulder left whose chest.

Time tilts to the future
but this is no reason for the imbalance of our life.
I met birds with burnt wings
like a group of insomniacs.

I met wrongly printed words, and there was
a strange geometry in their strokes and structure,
— few would know what is locked within.

卵石

——依靠感觉生存。
它感觉流水，
感觉其急缓及从属的年代，
感觉那些被命名为命运的船
怎样从头顶一一驶过。

依靠感觉它滞留在
一条河不为人知的深处，
某种飞逝的力量
致力于创造又痴迷取消，并以此
取代了它对岁月的感受。

——几乎已是一生。它把
因反复折磨而失去的边际
抛给河水，任其漂流并在远方成为
一条河另外的脚步声。

Pebble

— Depending on sensation to live,
it feels the water flowing,
feels the urgency and the epoch it belongs to,
feels those ships named fate
passing above its head, one by one.

Depending on sensation to remain
in the depth of an unknown river,
it possesses a fleeting power
to create and obsessively uncreate, by which
it is kept from feeling the passage of years.

— Almost for a lifetime. It throws
its edge, lost in repeated tortures,
to the river, letting it drift to become
the alternate footfall of a faraway river.

梦

总有人在我梦里出现,
一些熟悉或从未谋面的人。
总在梦里陌生的地方,目睹陌生的
城市、原野、怪物和深渊。

梦见的祖父是个农夫,我记不起
他旧军人的身份。
梦里的祖母如此年轻,她是从
一张旧照片上走下来的,彼时,
我还没有出生。
我梦见一群警察,他们来自荧屏,又像
来自某个古老的体系。他们
是怎样长途跋涉并准确地
找到了我的梦?

我梦见的老虎热爱鱼类,
一块草坪像个罪人。
美梦中没有神,噩梦里必有鬼,
我梦见过我会飞,却从未因此

Dream

I always dreamed of people
some familiar, some never met.
I always travelled to strange places, witnessing
strange cities, wilderness, monsters, and an abyss.

In my dream, my grandfather
was a farmer, not a veteran,
and my grandmother was so young,
right out of an old photo
from before I was born.
I dreamed of police officers from TV
or from an ancient system,
how would they travel so far to
enter my dream with such accuracy?

In my dream, the tiger is in love with fish,
a stretch of lawn is like a sinner.
In good dreams, no gods; in bad dreams, always ghosts.
I dreamed of flying, but never grew wings.

长出翅膀。而那与我梦里相逢的人
据说是假人,因为
他们死去多年,总想借助我的梦
重回已经不存在的光阴。

梦,是否也是种确凿的经历?
——它一直在篡改我的人生,甚至,
想把我从我的生活中带走。
从前的女友也曾来过,我是否该相信
我会再次被爱?
——当她离去,醒来的我
已近暮年,仍有与年轻时同样的伤悲。

And some people I met in my dreams
must have been mannequins,
for they had been dead for years
yet they tried to return to life by my dream.

Is the dream also a real experience?
— it has tampered with my life, even
tried to take me away from daily living.
My ex-girlfriend too visited me once in a dream;
should I believe that I would be loved by her again?
— when she left, I woke up as a middle-aged man
who harbored the same sadness as in youth.

见鬼

昨夜,老K从柳树下经过,
遇见一个漂亮的女鬼。
他说,她折下一根柳条,要他
把住址写在她的胸口上。

他写的,是隔壁一个游乐场的地址。

在这世上,有人会有艳遇,有人
会有厄运,还有人
就住在隔壁,彻夜难眠。

——其危险在于:
人有人行道,鬼有穿墙术。而且,
你是个心中有鬼的人,并可能

因此错过一个好结局。
对此,老K不作辩解。但他说,
如果有谁想试一试,他愿意
告诉你那棵柳树的位置。

Seeing a Ghost

Last night, Lao K passed under the willow tree.
and encountered a beautiful she-ghost.
He said that she broke a twig from the willow tree
and asked him to write his address on her chest.

Then he wrote the address of a theme park next door.

In this world, some people get to have an affair;
as for others, just a bit of bad luck, and those who
live next door will be sleepless all night.

— The real danger lies in this:
a living one has passageways to walk on,
a ghost has its methods to pass through the walls,
while you, a person with a ghost in your heart,

might miss out on a good ending.
Lao K made no excuse for this, but he said,
If anyone wants to give it a try, he is willing
to let you know the location of the willow tree.

光

案上的蜡烛,守着一寸寸矮下来的光。
对于煎熬,灯笼从不开口,对于
要在大风中不停地晃来晃去,
它抱紧内心里烧不完的寂静。
而盲者、脊背油亮的搬运工、从医院的座椅上
起身时眼前一黑的人……
你怎样把光递给他们?
悲伤慢于闪电,慢于石头的纹理,和一个在巷道里
爬行的少年。而火车在加速,飞快地
穿过隧道。钢轨上,溅起的火星硬如砂粒。而在
遥远乡间的祖屋里,父亲为了省钱,天黑后,
迟迟不肯打开电灯的开关,
——他习惯了黑暗,并把一只悬浮在
空中的灯泡,教导成了长夜的亲人。

Light

Candle on the desk guards the shortening light, inch by inch.
Lantern never complains of its ordeal,
made to sway endlessly in the heavy wind. It
holds the ever-burning stillness in its heart.
As for the blind man, the porter with glistening back,
and the one who fainted from the hospital seat...
how do you pass the light to them?
Grief is slower than lightning, slower than patterns in stone,
slower than a youth crawling in the alleyway.
Meanwhile the train is accelerating, hurtling fast
through the tunnel. The hard rails throw sparks
like sand grains.
Meanwhile in our ancestral home in a distant village,
to save money, my father refuses to turn on the light
— used to the darkness,
he raises a light bulb as family in the long night.

老手表

淘汰了的老手表
非常安静,锈迹
和珐琅壳上黯淡的光,都在证明
曾经有过的荒芜。但只须
拧紧发条,它马上就欢快地
走起来,忘记了过去的所有停顿。
若再拨正指针,就完全
与现在同步了,而若
不作校准,它则会接上原来的时间
继续跑,证实的是一段
已抛在我们身后的旧时光。
——曾经的事
不可能因此再发生一次,但它
一圈一圈跑得认真,并藉由我输入的
一小点气力,把曾
寄托在某个遗落世界里的迷宫,拖进
我们现在的生活中。

A Vintage Wristwatch

A vintage wristwatch is very quiet; flecks of rust
and the dim gleam on its enamel case
offer proof of a dissipated past. But you
only need to tighten its spring, and it will
run gaily and forget all the pauses in the past.
If you position the hands, it will
synchronize with the present time, but if you
forget to set it correctly; it will
continue to run from the original hour,
confirming a left-behind stretch of time.
— even so, whatever happened
will not happen again, but it
runs in diligent circles,
and with a bit of effort on my part,
drags a maze once grounded on a long-lost world
into our present life.

鸟在叫

鸟在叫,在树丛中。
北风的喘息,已有人把它
从窗玻璃上擦去。

——多少声音追随,飞掠向
另外的空间……
返回的,只是莫名的混响,
稀薄,模糊,不再有用。

粗大的木梁横于屋顶,沉默,稳定。
漫长一日,
由无数一晃而过的瞬间构成。

石栏、水、书橱……
都是被声音处理过的事物。

——我还是离那只鸟儿最近,
正站在
它用叫声编织的阴影中。

The Bird is Chirping

The bird is chirping in the woods.
The impalpable breath of north wind
has been wiped away from the window pane.

— many voices follow, flitting
toward another space ...
what comes back is just an inexplicable reverb,
thin, fuzzy, no longer useful.

The thick horizontal roofbeam is silent and stable.
A long day is made
by countless moments passing.

Stone fence, water, bookcase ...
are all processed by the sound.

— I am the one who stands nearest to that bird,
standing under the shadow
woven by the sound of chirping.

灯

一次是在谷底,他仰起头,深蓝的液体
在高处晃动,某种遗弃的生活如同
海底的石兽,时间,借助它们在呼吸。
"在这样的地方站得久了,
会长出鳃的。"他有了慌乱……
另一次是在山巅,几小块灯斑
像不明事物的胎记。他意识到,
所有的花瓣,都有扁平、不说话的身体。
——他在灯影里徘徊。有时,
走上黑暗中的楼梯,为了体验
严峻的切线边缘,某种激荡、
永远不可能被完成的旋律。
"光高于所有悬空的事物。"他发现,
恋人们接吻时,身体是半透明的。而且,
群山如果再亮些,真的会变成水母;但

Lamp

Once at the bottom of a valley, he looked at the liquid
azure high above in which there were
pulsations, an abandoned life form,
as if time were being measured by the breaths
of a stone beast at the bottom of the sea.
"One would grow fins
if one stood here too long." He felt panicky ...
Another time was from a peak, spots of lamplight
appeared like birthmarks on unknown objects.
As he wavered in a lamp's cone of light, he realized
that all petals are mute, their flesh lacks depth.
Sometimes, he climbed stairs in the dark
to experience the harsh tangential edge,
a stirring impulse…a forever-unfinished melody.
"Light is higher than all things that occupy space."
He found that lovers have translucent bodies
   when they are kissing;
and mountains would turn to jellyfish were they any brighter;

沉浸在黑暗中,也有不可捉摸的愉悦。
群星灿烂。这已是隔世的
另一天,不必要再证明什么是永恒。一盏
熄灭的灯也是那留下的灯,疲倦光线
在最后一瞬抓住的东西,藏着
必须为之活下去的秘密。

yet there's also an elusive pleasure of being immersed in
   the darkness.
Splendor of star clusters. Another day
in another world. No need to prove what is eternal.
A snuffed-out lamp is also the lamp that remains,
and the things caught at the last moment
by its weary rays
hide a secret we must go on living for.

树林

在一棵树和另一棵树之间,
有大片可以促膝的沉寂。
倚着树干说话的人,曾嗓音清晰。
当他起身——起风了,
无数话语,已同风声混在一起。

莫名的声音在林表喧响,
看林人的背影是粗糙的树皮。
他从暮色中归来,心中
藏着一把长柄斧的沉默。
刚刚,他出席过一个族人的葬礼。

大风把树林又拍打了一夜,
什么事物一转身,就落叶遍地?
鸟儿在不安的黎明中起身,掠过
催眠的光线、倒下的树,
以及随之被取消的一切。

Forest

Between one tree and another, there is
ample stillness to sit and exchange confidences.
The speaker leaning on a trunk had a distinct voice,
as he gets up — the wind blows,
countless words mingle with the wind.

An inexplicable voice murmurs at the forest's edge,
and the warden has a rough bark back.
He returns through the dusk, in his heart hiding
the stillness of a long-handled ax.
Moments ago, he attended the funeral of a tribesman.

Again the heavy wind blows the forest all night.
What strews fallen leaves the moment it turns about?
A bird wakes in the restless dawn, swooping
by hypnotic light, fallen trees
and all things canceled out in its aftermath.

墙

一堵墙出现，带着
黯淡的雨痕。几乎没有暖意。
它知道，它已在多数人视线之外。
让我记起，一个老家的人
也曾来这城里找我，到处打听我的住址。
（他年轻时的模样依稀浮现。）
而在遥远的地方，一堵墙
已不再被需要。拆了。必须
借助描述才能重新出现。
……扁豆架繁密的触丝晃动，阴影下
墙伸展着，像一段冥想。
——它有了某种意识，提前
预感到了那回忆它的人
将会赋予它的风声和悲伤。
——终于摒弃了声音，它伫立在
对虚无世界的倾听中。

The Wall

The wall appears, bearing dreary marks
of rain. Hardly a hint of warmth.
It knows that it's beyond sight of most people.
I recall that a fellow from my hometown
came to look for me in the city, asking for my address
everywhere.
(His youthful image comes faintly to mind.)
And in a distant place, the wall
no longer needed, has been demolished.
It only appears in a narrative.
...lush tendrils sway on broad-bean frames, in the shade
the wall stretches like a meditation.
— it had some kind of awareness, anticipating
the wind and misery conferred on it
by the person who would recall it.
— finally, it abandoned all sounds, standing
in heedfulness to the world of non-being.

老街

人群散后,我来这老街里走走,
陪街心的流水走走。
苦柳无言,花朵半明半暗,星光
是病人的秘密。
小庙和会馆都关了门,无人看见变幻。
蝉声疏落,斗拱的安静深于岁月的安静。
要走到一座老桥的拱顶上你才能
知道它在想什么。
酒肆喧闹,河流在黑暗中分岔,
红灯笼温暖的光,像来自前生,又像一种
可以延后支取的时间。

Old Street

After the crowd dispersed, I come to this old street,
walking along the stream down the middle.
Bitter willow wordless, flowers half-bright half-dim,
starlight holds the secrets of an invalid.
A small temple and guildhall are all closed,
and no one minds the change.
Sparse whirr of cicadas, the stillness of archway is deeper than passing years.
Only atop the rise of an old vaulted bridge,
would you know what it's thinking.
Noisy restaurant bar splits darkness over the river,
warm glow of red lanterns, as if from a past life, as if by deferred withdrawal of light.

老火车

火车飞驰,窗外,风景闪过。
在一列飞驰的火车上,车窗
什么也不打算拥有。

每个小站,都有人上车,有人
重新坐到车窗前。
我想起贪婪也能让人宁静,
一块玻璃也会心绪不宁。

老火车走走停停,
——我并没有从往事里挣脱出来。
当它吼叫,加速,那劝说你忘记的人,
都是人间的失败者。

季节晃动,带着玻璃的透明。
——失去你的音讯已很久了。大地
被留在铁道两旁,
这漫长的哑剧,不是火车,
铁轨才像更称职的演员。

Old Train

The train is speeding, scenery flashes by.
On a speeding train, the window
holds onto nothing.

At each small station, someone boards the train,
the others sit back, next to the window.
It strikes me that even greed could keep people quiet,
while a glass pane might make them restless.

The old train runs and stops.
— I haven't broken free from the past.
As it roars and speeds up, those who urge you to forget
are losers in the game of being human.

The swaying seasons have the transparency of glass.
— no word from you for a long time. The world
is left on both sides of the rails,
in this long pantomime, not the train
but the tracks are more suitable actors.

又一列火车迎面驰来。
它们多么有力,呼啸着,向我身后
刚刚经过的暮色里奔去。

Towards me, another train comes

robust, whistling, speeding

toward the dusk that just fell behind me.

陪父亲住院

穿白衣的人是天使,
你病得越重,她脚步越轻。所以,
父亲醒来后就不再说话。
——他在沉默中学习重新做人。

邻床是个半身不遂的汉子,
总用一只手在空中抓,
边抓边嘟囔:"别走……"
他老婆说,他看见了不该看的东西。
而医生的解读是:人在病中,
常会有些隐秘的约会。

手术台总是亮得刺眼。椅子上
坐着眼前阵阵发黑的人。
长廊幽深:一条
被我写进这首诗里的长廊,
像一条在人间摇晃的路,没有尽头,
拿不准自己要去哪里。

Staying with My Father at the Hospital

The woman in white is an angel.

the graver your illness, the lighter she treads.

so when my father woke up, he stopped talking,

— learned to be human again in his stillness.

Next bed, a half-paralyzed man, one hand

always clutching at the air, murmured, "Don't go..."

His wife said he saw something that shouldn't be seen.

But his doctor diagnosed differently:

In sickness, a man may often have a secret rendezvous.

The operating table is always dazzling bright.

Sitting in chairs are men who suffered fainting spells.

The corridor long and deep, written by me

into this poem, is like a road lurching through the

human sphere, endless and unsure where it's headed.

夜间，许多事物消失了。窗玻璃
像一面镜子，使病房门看上去
像悬浮在室外，从那里
出去的人，一转眼
消失在难测的黑暗中。

At night, many things vanished. The window
is a mirror making the door seem to float
beyond the sickroom. If you go out through it,
you would disappear into unpredictable darkness
in the blink of an eye.

初春

砖瓦厂里,老旧的拖拉机突然
发出轰鸣,喷吐浓烟,全身关节
喀吧作响,履带
扣紧尚未解冻的地面……
烟囱、枯草、坯房、树枝上的寒霜,都在震动中
猛然醒来。一辆
开始奋力前行的拖拉机,抖落积尘,着手解决
它和世界之间存在已久的问题。

Early Spring

In the brick factory, an old tractor suddenly
rumbles, thick smoke spurts, body joints
noisily clacking, treads grab
for traction on unthawed ground ...
chimney, hay, shed, and frost on branches
are all waking up in a sudden vibration.
The tractor strives to go forward, shakes off dust,
starting to fix its long-standing problem with the world.

窗

自那中间,一只无形的手
取走过一张又一张脸。

当你靠近,更多事物自它
周边移入,停在那里。
——仍像是第一次,月亮出发,要去
无法界定的年代里旅行。

光线有的迷惘,风没有;
形状关乎内涵。洞见多孔。

来回踱步者得到过
虚无的界线:从一侧
俘获的,在另一侧被放走。

而凝视的真谛是:站定,
在片面中重新确定一个中心……

现在,拉上窗帘吧,让那中心回到
自己的位置,或者,
不明白自己身在何处。

Window

From the window, an unseen hand
takes away one face after another.

As you get closer, more things move
into the window from its surroundings and stop there.
— just like the first time, when the moon set out,
travelling to an undefined year.

Some light is confusing, but not the wind;
A form is about content. The hole is porous.

The one who paces back and forth
has gotten to the border of the nothingness:
what is captured on one side is released on the other.

But the truth of gazing is: to stand still,
amid biases confirm a center once again...

Now, let us draw the curtains, let the center
return to its own position, or
admit that we don't know where we are.

石雕

说到底,一块石头对自己
也没有把握。
……谁手持斧凿,谁就能
重现历史被建造的方式。

曾藏在它体内的深刻现在是
豁显的表面……
正慢慢剥蚀,甚至,会在猝然一击中断折。
——当雕凿完成,意外,
或为时间所看重的耐心就去研究
它真正的内部。

一无所获:我们
从不曾于任何形象中得救。
蛮力过后,野草陪伴着它的寂静,
像无意识的真理。

Stone Sculpture

After all, a stone isn't quite
sure of itself.
......whoever holds an ax would
reshape history as he likes.

Profundity once hidden inside the stone
now shows on the surface......
slowly eroding, and even breaking apart at a blow.
— when the sculpture is completed, only by accident
or time-honored patience, will one study
its genuine inwardness.

Nothing to gain: we
have never been redeemed by any image.
After brute force, weeds stay with its stillness,
like an unconscious truth.

悬浮

水其实并不需要鱼,
但终其一生,水陪伴鱼就像陪着
某种反复思虑却一直
无所得的东西。

它护送鱼来到某个人心中,目睹它
成为一只渐渐适应了涡流的眼。
而它自身,任目光穿过,
不接纳注视。

鱼,总像悬浮在空无中。
——那空无收留了它,和簇拥着它的
受难般的宁静。

Suspension

Water never really needs fish.
But for its whole life, water stays with fish
as if to be near what it had longed for
but had never attained.

It escorts the fish to someone's heart, and witnesses
fish's gradual adaption to a swirling eye.
But water itself lets the gaze pass through,
does not accept any attention.

The fish seems suspended, as if in emptiness.
— The void accepts the fish, as well as
the tormented silence surrounding it.

涌泉

"你要穿过那黑暗,因为
所有事都不会真的消失。"

置身于变化,
但无法探究发生了什么。辨认中,
地心重力像一种
正在缓慢发育的智力。从那里,一个

仿佛隐藏着永恒的地方,
它被突然送回……

喷涌,因过于清冽以至于
无法用来讲述那经历。

Artesian Spring

"You must pass through the darkness, for
there is nothing that really disappears. "

Finding itself amidst changes,
unable to inquire what happened, it recognized
that gravity is a slow-developing intelligence.
From that point,

a place that seems to harbor eternity,
it was sent back suddenly…

A gushing spring, too clear
to tell what it experienced.

讲古的人

讲古的人在炉火旁讲古,
椿树站在院子里,雪
落满了脖子。
到春天,椿树干枯,有人说,
那是偷听了太多的故事所致。

炉火通红,贯通了
故事中黑暗的关节,连刀子
也不再寒冷,进入人的心脏时,暖洋洋,
不像杀戮,倒像是在派送安乐。

少年们在雪中长大了,
春天,他们饮酒,嫖妓,进城打工,
最后,不知所踪。

要等上许多年,讲古的人才会说,
他的故事,一半来自师传,另一半
来自噩梦——每到冬天他就会
变成一个死者,唯有炉火
能把他重新拉回尘世。

Storyteller

The storyteller told an ancient story by the stove.
An ailanthus tree stood in the yard,
    up to its neck in snow.
In the spring, the tree withered.
It eavesdropped on too many stories, said someone.

The stove burned bright red, soldering the dark joints
of the story. Even a knife takes on warmth
when plunged into a human heart, not so much
like a killing, more like delivery of merciful death.

Teenagers grew up in the snow.
In spring they drank, whored, labored in the city.
In the end, they vanished.

It takes years, the storyteller would say —
Half of his stories came from his master, the other half
    from his nightmares — every winter
he transformed into a dead man, only fire
could pull him back into the world of dust.

"因为,人在世上的作为不过是
为了进入别人的梦。"他强调,
"那些杜撰的事,最后
都会有着落(我看到他眼里有一盆
炭火通红),比如你
现在活着,其实在很久以前就死去过。
有个故事圈住你,你就
很难脱身。
但要把你讲没了,也容易。"

He insisted, "Everything we do in the world
is to enter others' dreams. "
"Those fictions will be shown for what they are. "
   (In his eyes, a pot of charcoal glowed.)
"For example, you may be alive today,
but in fact, you died long ago. If a story
entraps you, you will have a hard time escaping.
But it's also not difficult to make you disappear ."

剧情

戏台老旧。留住某些结局,
必须使用吊过的嗓子。
——抛出的水袖无声翻卷,其中
藏着世间最深的沉寂。

——有兰花指,未必有春天;
有小丑,则必有欢乐。
有念白,天,也许真的就白了。年月
长过一代又一代观众,却短于
半个夜晚。万水千山仍只是
一圈小碎步,使苦难看上去
比欢乐更准确。

——愤怒是你的,也是我的。
悲伤,所有人来分它,就会越分越多……
最后,散尽的繁华都交给
一声叹息来收拾。

Plot

The stage is rickety. To preserve certain endings
you must use a trained voice.
— the flowing sleeves were quietly rolled up,
hoarding the most profound solitude in the world.

— one who has orchid-fingers may not arouse springtime;
but a clown will assure merriment.
After blank verses, the sky may turn to be blank.
Time is longer than the generations of audiences
but shorter than half a night.
Circling the stage with gliding steps, your movements
passed over mountains and rivers, making misery
seem more apt than merriment.

— Fury was yours, as it was mine.
Sadness was multiplied if shared by all audiences...
In the end, all prosperity must conclude
with a simple sigh.

那在后台调油彩的人最懂得:脸,
要变成脸谱,
才不会在锣鼓的催促中消失。

The backstage makeup master knows better: face
must be covered by face mask, for it not to disappear
in the urging of gongs and drums.

后主

他喜欢投壶,饮酒,填词,把美人
认作美狐。
"雪是最大的迷宫。"他喜欢旧句子中
别人不曾察觉的意义。
——河山不容讨论,但在诗中是个例外。
他喜欢指鹿为马
——雪给他造出过一匹马。
"雪并不单调,因为白包含的
总是多于想象。"
雪继续下,雪底的雕栏像输掉的筹码。
一个压低了的声音在说:
美哦,让人耽留的美,总是美如虚构!

Last Emperor

He likes wine, lyric poems, and to play pitch-pot.
He likes to think of a beautiful woman as a beautiful fox.
"Snow is the largest maze."
He likes the hidden meaning of old verses.
— Mountains and rivers cannot be discussed
except in poetry.
He likes to treat deer as horses
— snow has made a horse for him.
Snow is not dull.
The whiteness is always fuller than imagined.
Snow keeps falling, the carved railing underneath
like a losing stack of chips, sighs a low voice,
Beauty, O, enchanting beauty
is always as beautiful as fiction.

北风

戏台上,祝英台不停地朝梁山伯说话。
日影迟迟。所有的爱都让人着急。

那是古老南国,午睡醒来,花冠生凉,
半生旁落于穿衣镜中。瓷瓶上的蓝,
已变成某种抽象的譬喻。

"有幸之事,是在曲终人散前化为蝴蝶……"
回声依稀,老式木桌上,手
是最后一个观众,
——带着人间不知晓的眷顾。

North Wind

On the stage, Zhu Yingtai kept talking to Liang Shanbo .
The shadow of the sun moved slowly
All who were in love were prone to anxiety.

In the old southland, petals breathed coolness as a siesta ended.
By the dressing mirror, half a life fell away.
Blue glaze on porcelain had become an abstract metaphor.

"How lucky to change into a butterfly before the song ends and lovers part..."
echoes grew faint, an old wooden table, a hand
were the last audience,
— bringing nostalgia not known to human beings.

地图鱼

把一个词拆开,拆成地图和鱼,
地图就将变大,
装得下许多国家的恩仇。
鱼则将变冷,
收留下一枚暗铁的忧愤。

彼时,鱼还不是宠物,许多事
都有另外的开始。比如:
地图在匣中安静地卷着,一条河边
有人击筑,有人高歌,某种
无名无姓的鱼在水里
游来游去,摆动着
与江山无关的斑斓纹理。

彼时,地图和鱼都不能
用来观赏。匕首也不能:它们
或藏身地图,或藏身鱼腹。
而一腔热血藏在
远行人体内:他衣袂飘拂,背影
逐渐模糊。一阵北风,
已提前把他的头颅取走。

Map Fish

Take apart a phrase, reduce it to a map and a fish.
The map would become large, large enough
to contain the enmities between countries.
The fish would become cold, cold enough
to swallow the indignation of dark iron.

At that time, a fish was not yet a pet, many things
had a different kind of beginning, for instance:
The map lay quietly rolled-up in its holder; by a river,
some were striking gongs, some were singing,
a nameless fish swam about, undulating
its mottled skin, which had nothing to do
with the territory of any land.

At that time, neither map nor fish were intended
for viewing pleasure; the dagger was not either.
One was hidden in the map, one in the fish belly,
as was boiling blood inside a man far from home:
robe fluttering, the shape of his back blurring,
his head had already been taken off
by a slashing gust of north wind.

雅鲁藏布江

白云飞往日喀则,
大水流向孟加拉。
昨日去羊湖,一江怒涛迎面,
今天顺流而下,水里的石头也在赶路。
乱峰入云,它们仍归天空所有。
——我还是在人间,
我要赶去墨脱城,要比这流水跑得快,
要赶在一块块石头的前面。

Yaruzangbu River

White clouds fly towards Rigezhe,
The great river flows towards Bangladesh.
Yesterday I went to Yang Lake, where raging water greeted me.
Today I go down the river, where stones too are rushing.
Thrusting into the clouds, the chaotic peaks are
still under the sky's dominion
— and I still belong to the earth.
I must hurry to Motuo City, must run faster than the flowing river,
must arrive earlier than this and that stones.

仙居观竹

雨滴已无踪迹,乱石横空。
晨雾中,有人能看见满山人影,我看见的
却是大大小小的竹子在走动。
据说此地宜仙人居,但劈竹时听见的
分明是人的惨叫声。
竹根里的脸,没有刀子取不出;
竹凳吱嘎作响,你体内又出现了新的裂缝。
——惟此竹筏,能把空心扎成一排,
产生的浮力有顺从之美。
闹市间,算命的瞎子摇动签筒,一根根
竹条攒动,是天下人的命在发出回声。

Viewing Bamboo at the Immortal's Abode

Where raindrops vanish, jumbled rocks jut into air.
In the morning mist, someone sees a mountain
full of people, yet I see only
the movement of small and large bamboos.
It's said that this place is suitable for immortals,
but I heard a man's howling as the knife split a bamboo.
With knife, you can get any face out of a bamboo.
Creaking of bamboo stool, new cracks appear in your body.
— only a raft can tie the hollowness into a row,
giving rise to buoyancy, the beauty of obedience.
In the market, a fortune teller shakes a tube-full of lots,
one by one they pop up — the rattling bamboo sticks —
echoing fates of all human beings in the world.

嘉峪关外

我知道风能做什么,我知道己所不能。
我知道风吹动时,比水、星辰,更为神秘。
我知道正有人从风中消失,带着喊叫、翅、饱含热
　力的骨骼。
多少光线已被烧掉,我知道它们,也知道
人与兽,甚至人性,都有同一个源泉的夜晚。
我的知道也许微不足道。我知道的寒冷也许微不足道。
在风的国度,戈壁的国度,命运的榔头是盲目的,
这些石头不祈祷,只沉默,身上遍布痛苦的凹坑。
——许多年了,我仍是这样一个过客:
比起完整的东西,我更相信碎片。怀揣
一颗反复出发的心,我敲过所有事物的门。

Outside Jayu Pass

I know what the wind can do that I cannot.
I know when the wind blows,
more mysterious than water and stars.
I know who is vanishing in the wind with his yell, his wings and burning bones.
How much light is burned out? I know.
And I also know that humans and animals,
even human natures share a single source of night.
My knowledge might be slim and my awareness of cold might be slight.
In the kingdom of wind and the Gobi, destiny's hammer is blind.
These stones don't pray, reman silent, covered by dents of pain
— for years, I am just a passerby:
I believe in fragments more than the whole.
With a traveler's heart
I have knocked at the door of all things.

春风斩

河谷伸展。小学校的旗子
噼啪作响。
有座小寺,听说已走失在昨夜山中。

牛羊散落,树桩孤独,
石头里,住着一直无法返乡的人。
转经筒转动,西部多么安静。仿佛
能听见地球轴心的吱嘎声。

风越来越大,万物变轻,
这漫游的风,带着鹰隼、沙砾、碎花瓣、
歌谣的住址和前程。

风吹着高原小镇的心。
春来急,屠夫在洗手,群山惶恐,
湖泊拖着磨亮的斧子。

Spring Wind Beheading

River valley stretches out. A flag at the small school
snaps loud. Last night, I heard a little temple
went missing in the mountains.

Cattle and sheep scatter, a lone stump stands.
Inside of stones lives a man who will never return home.
A prayer wheel is turning — how quiet the western world
as if we can hear the earth grinding on its axis.

The wind blows harder and harder, making all things lighter.
It carries falcons, gravel, broken petals,
the address of a song, the road ahead.

It sways the heart of a small town on the plateau.
Spring arrives in a hurry. Butcher washes his hands.
    Mountains panic.
Lakes drag a honed ax.

星

旅馆小院的墙角里,放着一堆陶罐,
一道道裂纹,正穿过愚钝者缓慢的余生……

果树在野外摇晃,每颗果子里
都住着一颗星;每颗星里,都住着失踪已久的人。
挂在墙上的壁钟有时会
咔嚓一响,吃掉它等待已久的东西。

鸟雀飞,山顶发蓝,空气中
有时会充满模糊的絮语,可一阵北风,
就能把所有嘴唇合拢。

破旧的陶罐,也许能认出某些人的原身。
但没有一种语言,能描述星星
一颗一颗,从天空中褪去的那种宁静,那种
你刚刚醒来,不知怎样开口说话的宁静。

Star

In the corner of a small hotel courtyard,
a pile of clay pots rests,
lines of cracks, passing through the rest of a fool's life...

Fruit trees rattling in the wild, in each fruit
lives a star; in each star, lives a long-lost man.
The wall clock, sometimes, makes a sudden sound,
swallowing whatever it has been waiting for.

Birds are flying, mountain top blue, in the air,
broken words full. But a gush of north wind
would seal all lips.

From those worn clay pots, you may recognize
    someone's origin in the past.
But no language can describe the stillness
when stars faint from the sky, one by one,
and you wake up, tongue-tied.

闻笛

猛虎跑过未知的年代,
洪水潜入经卷,和更早的生活。
沙棘刺坚硬,当归花是失而复得的礼物。
接骨木沉沉的,仿佛
有种忧伤已得到安慰:让它枝叶舒展的
不是水,是蓄积已久的苦痛。

在郎木寺外的山崖下,听见
一阵飘忽的笛声,仿佛来自某个遥远、未知的口唇。
它吹着蓬草,吹着干彻的了悟,
吹着失败者,向他心中无人收拾的刀斧致意。
小沙弥的袍子又大又宽松,笛声
吹着他,向他不谙世事的清新致意。

Listening to a Flute

Tiger runs past an unknown era,
Flood sneaks into scripture scrolls and bygone living.
Buckthorn spines are stiff, and angelica flower is a
    regained gift.
Bone-setting herb is immersed, as if in solace for sadness:
Only accumulated pain, not water,
causes its leaves to stretch open.

Outside Langmu Temple, under the cliff, I hear
rambling flute sounds, as if from a distant, unknown lip,
blow through grass and dried-out enlightenment, blow
    on a loser,
saluting sharp blades in his heart that no one is there to
    look after.
Young monk's robe and loose, flute sounds
play to him, saluting his innocent youth.

采药人

在半山腰遇到采药人,
他坐在那儿歇息,草药上沾着新泥
和隐秘的悲悯。

他在抽烟。熟悉药性的目光
有种疲惫的淡漠。让我想起
山下小镇里简陋的药铺,以及
许多噼啪作响的小抽屉。

病榻、叩首者、山羊平静的脸,它们
总会在一阵风中重逢,在一枚
秤砣冰冷的心中重逢。
——太多的人已在岁月中走散,
带着预感和祈祷的低语。

面对呼唤,希望和疑虑都有迟疑的脚步。
老旧、前世般的药篓,越来越像
一个懂得了艰难时世的人。

Herb Picker

Midway up the hill, I met a herb picker.
He was resting, the herbs stained with fresh mud
and private compassion.

Smoking, his glance so well-versed in powers of herbs,
showed a tired aloofness. He reminded me of
a single pharmacy in a small town at the foothill
and many squeaky, doll-sized drawers.

Sickbed, bows of supplication, a calm-faced goat
one can always meet again in a gust of wind
in a heart with cold, calculating scale.
— amid passing years, so many people parted ways,
with whispers holding omens and prayers.

In the face of a summons, hopes and doubts hesitate
   to respond.
The worn herb basket, like a revenant, more and more
resembles a person too well-acquainted with hard times.

沙漠

——这从消逝的时间中释放的沙,
捧在手中,已无法探究发生过什么。
每一粒都那么小,没有个性,没有记忆,也许
能从指缝间溜走的就是对的。

狂热不能用来解读命运,而无边荒凉
属于失败者。
只有失去在创造自由,并由
最小的神界定它们的大小。而最大的风
在它们微小的感官中取消了偏见。

又见大漠,
又要为伟大和永恒惊叹。
而这一望无际的沙,却只对某种临时性感兴趣。
沙丘又出现在地平线上。任何辉煌,到最后,
都由这种心灰意懒的移动来完成。

Desert

— This sand, released in the elapsing of time.
You hold it in your palm, unable to probe what
happened. Each grain is so tiny,
lacking character and memory; perhaps it's better
to let it slip through your fingers.

You can't interpret fate by frenzied passion;
endless desolation belongs to the defeated.
Only through loss does it create freedom
and let the smallest god define the size of the desert.
Yet the stiffest wind erases the bias of its small organs.

Again, I see the desert. Again, I must marvel
at its greatness and eternity. Yet the endless sand
is only interested in a fleeting moment.
Dunes again emerge on the horizon. Any glory,
in the end, must come about by such resigned motion.

篝火

手鼓急促,花朵灼热。
天黑透了,胡杨林在黑暗中静静地
守着新的光源。

手鼓在响,一条大河在天空中转弯。
——如此良宵,祈祷的人,饮酒的人,从天堂上
下来的人,大家围在一起歌唱……
火光耀动,穆塞莱斯闪着光。

多年前我就告诉过你,心怀伤痛者
必眼噙热泪。
多年后我还会告诉你,走过新疆你并不孤单,
爱如粗砂,如火中取栗。

Bonfire

Crescendo of tambourine, flowers ablaze.
Darkness has fallen, a quiet grove of poplar trees
Is watching over a new source of the light.

Loud beats of tambourine, a great river turns in the sky.
— such a fine night...supplicants, drinkers, new arrivals
from heaven, all singing together...
Bonfire flaring, cups of Moselle gleaming.

Years ago I told you, if the broken-hearted ones
come, their eyes will surely swim with tears.
Years later I will tell you, you are not alone in Xinjiang.
Rough like sand, love is,
like taking a chestnut from the bonfire.

源头

明亮的事物总漫不经心。
河边,戴头巾的少女在洗涤织物。
木舟划向树林。马的鬃毛,也像光芒一样流泻在水中。

也许,这就是我们早已失去的时辰,
像镜子、新鲜的日出。欢乐,像藉由浪费产生的涟漪。

——我也曾以为,那错过、忽略的,都能
凭借奔腾的争斗取回。
可无数浪涛已平静下来,带着对不在场事物的依恋。
静谧水湾收留了倒影,也收留了
我们一路丢弃的艰辛。

The Source

Bright things are always careless.
By the river, the head-scarfed girl washes her clothes.
A boat is poled toward woods. A horse's mane trails like
 light rays in the water.

Perhaps this is an hour we lost long ago,
like a mirror, a new sunrise, joy, and ripples made by
 what we waste.

— I once believed that what I'd missed or ignored
could be regained by strong effort.
but countless waves have grown calm, nostalgic for
what is no longer present.
A quiet bay takes in reflected images, as well as
the hardships we abandoned along the way.

平武读山记

我爱这一再崩溃的山河,爱危崖
如爱乱世。
岩层倾斜,我爱这
犹被盛怒掌控的队列。

……回声中,大地
猛然拱起。我爱那断裂在空中的力,
以及它捕获的
关于伤痕和星辰的记忆。

我爱绝顶,也爱那从绝顶
滚落的巨石一如它
爱着深渊:一颗失败的心,余生至死,
爱着沉沉灾难。

Reading the Mountains in Pingwu

I love the mountains and rivers that once again
collapse, and love the dangerous cliffs
just like troubled times. Rocks tilted.
I love the order that is controlled by fury.

...In an echo, the earth
suddenly arched. I love the force broken
in the air and the memory of the scars and stars
it captured.

I love the mountain top but also love the giant rock
rolling down from the top
as if for its love of the abyss: For the rest of life, a
    failed heart
loves great disasters.

星相

老木匠认为,人间万物都是上天所赐,
他摸着木头上的花纹说,那就是星相。
我记得他领着徒弟给家具刷漆的样子,某种蓝
白天时什么都能刷掉,到了夜晚,
则透明,回声一样稀薄。
他死时繁星满天。什么样的转换
在那光亮中循环不已?
能将星空和人间搭起来的还有
风水师,他教导我们,不可妄植草木,打井,拆迁,
或把
隔壁的小红娶回家,因为,这有违天意。
而我知道的是,老家具在不断掉漆,
我们的掌纹、额纹……都类似木纹,类似
某种被利斧劈开的东西。
——眺望仍然是必须的,因为
老透了的胸怀,嘈杂过后就会产生理智。

The Movement of Stars

The old carpenter believes all things in the world are
   God's gifts.
He traces the grain of the wood and says:
This is the movement of stars.
I remember how he taught his apprentice to paint furniture
a shade of blue brushing over anything in the day
but at night, it became transparent, thin as an echo.
The sky was full of stars when he died —
what is transformed into that endless cycle of light?
A fengshui master can also connect stars with the world.
He warned us not to plant trees randomly, drill wells
demolish houses, move house
or marry Xiao Hong next door
but I know the paint on old furniture always peels off.
Our palm lines, forehead wrinkles...like the grain
of the wood split by an ax
— It's crucial to look upward.
After a period of noise, a ripe mind is bound to produce
   wisdom.

"你到底害怕什么?" 当我自问,星星们也在
朝人间张望,但只有你长时间盯着它,
它才会眨眼——它也有不解的疑难,类似
某种莫名的恐惧需要得到解释。

"What're you afraid of?" I ask myself. The stars
gaze down at us, too. If you gaze back long enough,
they will blink — with their perplexities, like
an unfathomable fear that needs to be named.

水龙头

弯腰的时候,不留神,
被它碰到了额头。

很疼。我直起身来,望着
这块铸铁,觉得有些异样。
它坚硬、低垂,悬于半空,
一个虚空的空间,无声环绕
弯曲、倔强的弧。

仿佛是突然出现的,
——这一次,它送来的不是水,
而是它本身。

Faucet

Bent over, careless
I hit my forehead on it.

It really hurts. I straighten up and examine
the piece of cast iron, somewhat strange,
hard, drooping, hanging in midair,
a void of space, surrounded by silence,
a bend, a stubborn arc.

It suddenly appears,
— but this time, instead of water,
it sends itself.

玛曲

吃草的羊很少抬头,
像回忆的人,要耐心地
把回忆里的东西
吃干净。

登高者,你很难知道他望见了什么。
他离去,丢下一片空旷在山顶。

我去过那山顶,在那里,
我看到草原和群峰朝天边退去。
—— 黄河从中流过,
而更远的水不可涉,
更高的山不可登。

更悠长的调子,牧人很少哼唱,
一唱,就有牦牛抬起头来,
—— 一张陌生人的脸孔。

Maqu

Grazing sheep rarely raise their heads.
Like people ruminating on the past, they must
lick clean the bowl of memory, patiently.

It is hard to know what a climber sees
at the top of the mountain,
and he leaves behind an empty space.

I've been to the top of the mountain.
I've seen the peaks and prairies receding
   toward the horizon.
— the Yellow River flows between,
no river longer than this river,
no mountain higher than this mountain.

Shepherds seldom hum the longer melody.
If they sing, a yak will raise its head
— a stranger's face.

猫

我写作时,
猫正在我的屋顶上走动,
没有一点声响。

当它从高处跳下,落地,
仍然没有声响。
它松开骨骼,轻盈,像一个词
完成了它不可能完成的事,并成功地
没有引起我们的注意。

它蹲在墙头、窗台,或椅子上。
它玩弄一个线团,哦,修辞之恋:浪费了
你全部心神的复杂性,看上去,
简单,愉悦,无用。

它喜欢在白天睡大觉,像个它者。
当夜晚来临,世界
被它拉进了放大的瞳孔。
那是离开了我们的视野去寻求
新的呈现的世界……

Cat

While I am writing,
a cat strides quietly on my roof,
not a hint of sound.

It jumps down, lands on the ground,
not a hint of sound.
Loose-limbed and agile, like a word it manages
to do what can't be done, and succeeds
at not attracting our attention.

It squats on a wall or windowsill or chair,
playing with a ball of yarn. O penchant for rhetoric,
wasting all your intelligence on the complexity
   of what now seems to be
simple, pleasant, and useless.

It loves daylong naps, as if uninvolved.
When night comes, it pulls the world
into its enlarged pupils,
and deserts our glance to seek
a newly emerged world...

这才是关键：不是我们之所见而是
猫之所见。
不是表达，而是猫那藏起了
所有秘密的呼噜或喵的一声。

它是这样的存在：不可解。
它是这样的语言：经过，带着沉默，
当你想写下它时，
它就消失了。

That's the crucial thing: not what we saw,
but what a cat saw; not what we
expressed, but what secrets
a cat harbored in its snore or a meow.

It is such a being: unexplainable.
It is such a verse: fleeting, holding silence,
then you want to write it down,
it evaporates.

风中的事

风在吹,船在漂移。
廊柱间,蛛网仿佛废弃的罗盘。

风在吹,虚线离开实体,
有人在说话,图案与心灵不对称,
光站在针尖上,旗帜远去。

风在吹。风中的事总是
有了开始却没有结局。
墙上的吉他:遥远的星座,
街边的邮筒:穿雨衣的男子。

风在吹,从空旷的广场上经过时
突然加速,将高大的悬铃木猛力摇撼。
……一瞬间它认出了,那些
正在树干里挣扎的人。

Things in the Wind

Wind is blowing, a boat is drifting.
Between verandah columns, a spider web
like a compass abandoned.

Wind is blowing. The dotted line leaves the entity.
Someone is talking, picture and heart mismatching;
Light stands on the needle's tip, the flag gone far away.

Wind is blowing. After the beginning,
things in the wind go on with no end.
Guitar on the wall, constellation far away,
Postbox by the street, man in a raincoat.

Wind is blowing, over an empty square,
suddenly quickening, violently tossing
   the tall sycamore trees.
...Just then, within tree trunks, it recognizes
the ones who are in the throes of struggle.

窗前

当我们在窗前交谈,我们相信,
有些事,只能在我们的交谈外发生。

我们相信,在我们目力不及的地方,
走动着陌生人。他们因为
过着一种我们无法望见的生活而摆脱了
窗口的限制。

当他们回望,我们是一群相框中的人,
而那空空、无人的窗口,
正是耗尽了眺望的窗口。

我们看到,城市的远端,
苍穹和群山拱起的脊背
像一个个问号:过于巨大的答案,
一直无法落进我们的生活中。

当我们在长长的旅行后归来,
嵌入窗口的风景,
再也无法从玻璃中取出。

At the Window

As we talk at the window, we believe that some things
would only occur outside of our conversation.

We believe that in an unseen place,
strangers are walking about. Their lives are beyond
where our vision can reach, so they are freed
from the window's constraints.

As they look back, we are figures in a picture frame,
and that empty, deserted windowpane —
in itself — is what does all the gazing.

We lay eyes on the far edge of the city
and the arched back of sky and mountains
like a series of question marks: an answer too huge
to fit into our lives.

When we return from a long trip,
that scenery embedded in our window
can no longer be retrieved from the glass.

在南京

在南京,
我喜欢听静海寺的钟声。如果

稍稍对喧哗做出避让,
比如避开八点钟,
我会去颐和路,或珞珈路上走走。
我捡拾过落叶,时间夹缝中
身份不明的人寄来的信函。

有时在旋转餐厅上
俯瞰,城市如星空,那些
或明或暗的中心,都在旋转,缓缓
发生位移。

在江边,或石象路上,
眼前的事物,总像带着未知的远方。
眺望钟山,那亭台、苍翠峰顶,
仿佛都含着世界的尽头。

In Nanjing

In Nanjing, I love to listen
to Jinghai Temple bell. If I decide

to evade the noise of crowds,
such as by staying away at eight o'clock,
I would walk on Yihe Road, or Luojia Road.
I've picked up fallen leaves, in a crack of time,
letters sent by someone unidentified.

Sometimes in the revolving restaurant
I would overlook the city, like a starry expanse
its changeable centers, bright or dim, all rotating
and slowly shifting.

By the river, or on the stone elephant road,
all things presented portend an unknown future.
I gaze on Zhong Mountain, where pavilions and verdant heights
seem to hold in themselves the far end of the world.

航班晚点

北方暴雨。天空一片空旷。
落在地上的雨管住了天上的事。

候机大厅拥堵,雨,
下在人的心里。我从许多多云的脸,
瞥见了他们内心的闪电。

我的母亲说:不要急。
一辈子她都喜欢说:不要急。
我是听话的,而她的心脏、血压、血栓……
都不怎么听话。
有次我见她难受地用手按住心口,
像在安抚另一个孩子。

母亲,我不急。
去吸烟室、洗手间的时候,
我已反复叮嘱过自己:不要急!
千里之外,你躺在医院的病床上,
——母亲,也许窗外落下的那不是雨,
只是命运的又一种坏脾气。

Flight Delayed

In the north, heavy rain. The sky, a big blank.
Rain falling on earth decides what happens in the sky.

In a crowded waiting hall, the rain
falls into everyone's heart. From many cloudy faces,
I see the lightning in their hearts.

My mother says, DON'T WORRY.
She always likes to say, DON'T WORRY.
I'm an obedient son, but her heart, blood pressure,
blood clots...don't behave all that well.
Once I saw her hands pressing her chest in discomfort,
as if to appease a child.

Mother, I'm not in a hurry.
I will go to the smoking room, to the bathroom.
I will repeatedly tell myself: DON'T WORRY!
A thousand miles away, you're lying in a hospital bed
— Mother, maybe what is falling outside the window
is not rain but a temper tantrum of destiny.

某园,闻古乐

山脊如虎背。
—— 你的心曾是巨石和细雨。

开满牡丹的厅堂,
曾是家庙、大杂院、会所,现在
是个演奏古乐的大园子。
—— 腐朽的木柱上,龙
攀援而上,尾巴尚在人间,头
消失于屋檐下的黑暗中:它尝试着
去另外的地方活下去。

琴声迫切,木头有股克制的苦味。
—— 争斗从未停止。
歇场的间隙,有人谈起盘踞在情节中的
高潮和腥气。剧中人和那些
伟大的乐师,
已死于口唇,或某个隐忍的低音……

当演奏重新开始,
一声鼓响,是偈语在关门。

In a Garden, Listening to Ancient Music

Ridgeline like a tiger's back
— your heart used to be a boulder and a drizzle.

A peony-blossomed hall
used to be a family shrine, a courtyard, a clubhouse,
now a large performance center for ancient music.
— winding around a rotting wooden pillar,
a dragon clambers, its tail still in this world, the head
vanished in the darkness under the eaves:
to try to live in another world.

Urgent the strings, bitterness suppressed in the wood.
— the battle never stops.
During the break, someone spoke of the bloody tang
and climax in the plot line. Characters in the play and
those great musicians
had already died on the lips, or subsided into low bass...

As the show resumed, a bang of the drum
was the door to a verse slamming.

邻居

邻居养鸟,不养鸡。
邻居养狗,牵着它散步。

我有仁慈的邻居,
他养花种草,脾气不好,但坦白,
精通精神疗法。
当他用竹竿敲打树上的黄叶,
秋天就会死去。

我的邻居把别针别在袖口上,
把花园改成菱形。
到了一定的年龄,他就说谎,
并真诚地笑着,
仿佛谎言和笑容都不够用。

我的邻居养猫,让猫,
在夜晚出行,替他去查看这城市。
——控制黑暗的,

My Neighbor

My neighbor keeps a bird, but no chicken.
He walks his dog often.

My kind-hearted neighbor
grows flowers and herbs. He is temperamental
but frank and good at psychotherapy.
When he beats yellow leaves from the tree with a
bamboo stick, autumn will die.

My neighbor wears a pin on his cuff
and redesigned his garden in a diamond shape.
When he reaches a certain age, he tells lies
but smiles sincerely
as if both lie and smile are not good enough.

My neighbor has a cat. He lets his cat
go out at night and patrol the city for him.
— that which controls the darkness

是一种没有声息的脚爪。
我的邻居鼾声阵阵,
对这世界了如指掌。

is a set of claws that make no sound.

My neighbor snores and knows the world

as if in the palm of his hand.

明月

1

——记忆的镣铐。
对于越狱者,天空过于开阔了。

低处,有个相反的国度,
明了一切的水,唱着安魂曲。

2

它躯体的一部分提前离开,悄悄
去了未来。

——那是用于占卜的明月,
当缺失的部分慢慢返回,从远方
带来了不为人知的消息。

Bright Moon

1

— The fetters of memory.
The sky is too vast for a jailbreaker.

In low places, there must be a different empire,
where water is suffused with light, a requiem is sung.

2

The bodily part of it left earlier, went quietly
into to the future.

— that was the moon used for divination,
when the missing part gradually returns, from a distance,
it brings a message unknown to many.

姜里村

一个小村,一片湖,偶有旅人。
去年在这里,我看见过一个溺死的老者,
沉在水中,竖直,像个日本玩偶。
他的儿子从村庄那头赶过来打捞他,
出水时,他身子很重,滑回水里多次,好像
还没有死,不愿离开那水。
他的儿子面色铁青,看不出一丝慌乱,手也有力。
哦,痛哭之前,还有那么多
需要咬紧牙关才能做的事。
后来,在他被拖走的地方,水渍
像一块继续扩大的胎记。
我站在那里,左边是老旧庭院,
右边是凶水;左边是破败的安宁,右边,
一个平静的镜面在收拾
村庄的倒影,和死亡留下的东西。

Jiangli Village

A small village, a lake, a few travelers.
Last year, an old man drowned,
submerged in the water, corpse vertical like a Japanese doll.
His son rushed from the village to salvage the corpse,
he was heavy and slipped back into the water several times
as if still not dead, not willing to leave the water.
His dark-faced son, not showing panic, grabbed hold
    powerfully.
O no time to cry yet, grit your teeth,
there are so many things you must do.
Later, where the corpse was dragged away,
the water stain, like a birthmark, continued to expand.
I stood there, to my left an old courtyard,
to my right the fateful water; to my left was broken
    tranquility,
to my right a still mirror reflecting the village,
and all things left by death.

鱼化石

石头是本糟糕的书,一页一页,
很难被揭开……
——而它是被顺便发现的,卡在

另外的叙述中,既非石头,亦非鱼。
——它知道自己打断不了什么,就慢慢
变成了意义不明的物种,带着
只有它自己能记住的。

Fish Fossil

What a terrible book the stone is, page after page,
hard to open
— but it was found by accident, in the midst of

other narratives, neither about stone, nor about fish.
— It knows that it won't be able to break off anything,
so it gradually becomes a vague species, standing for
what it alone can remember.

蟋蟀

蟋蟀一代代死去。
鸣声如遗产。

——那是黑暗的赠予。
当它们暂停鸣叫,黑暗所持有的
仿佛更多了。

——但或者
蟋蟀是不死的,你听到的一声
仍是最初的一声。
——古老预言,帮我们解除过
无数黄昏浓重的焦虑。

当蟋蟀鸣叫,黑夜如情感。或者,
那是一台旧灵车:当蟋蟀们
咬紧牙关格斗,断折的
头颅、大腿,是从灵车上掉落的零件。

——午夜失眠时,有人采集过
那激烈的沉默。

Cricket

Crickets died, generation after generation,
leaving their chirping as an legacy.

— That was the gift from the darkness.
When they pause, the darkness
seems to grow.

— But
perhaps crickets didn't die, what you heard
was the FIRST chirping.
— ancient prophecy helps us to dispel
many thick, dusky anxieties.

When crickets are chirping, the dark night is like an emotion, or,
like an old hearse: as crickets
grit teeth and duel with each other, broken
skulls and thighs are parts falling from the hearse.

— In midnight insomnia, someone collected
that intense silence.

"又一个朝代过去了,能够信任的
仍是长久的静场之后
那第一声鸣叫。"而当
有人从远方返回,并不曾带来
胜利者的消息。
但他发现,他、出租车的背部,
都有一个硬壳——在肉体的
规划中,欲望
从没打算满足命运的需求。

据说,蟋蟀的宅院
是废墟和草丛里唯一的景观。
但当你走近,蟋蟀
会噤声:静场仍是难解的密码。
当你长久站立,鸣声会再起,带着小小、
谶语的国向远方飘移。所以,

清醒的灵魂是对肉体的报复:那是
沸腾的蟋蟀、挣脱了
祖传的教训如混乱
心跳的蟋蟀,甚至
在白日也不顾一切地鸣叫,像发现了
真理的踪迹而不愿放弃的人。

"Another dynasty has passed, after a long silence, still
nothing can be trusted except the FIRST chirping."
And when someone returned from afar,
he brought no message from the victor.
But then he found: he and the taxi's hindmost part,
had grown a hard shell — in a plan of flesh,
desire never intended to meet the needs of fate.

It is said that the cricket's house
is the only sight amid the ruins and grass.
But when you approach, crickets
would stop chirping: their silence is still an enigma.
When you stand for a long time, the sound will
start again; it will drift away, carrying off the land
of singing girls and repentant prayers. And so,

a sober soul is a revenge on the flesh, which is
an effervescent cricket, a cricket that breaks free
from the arrhythmia of ancestral doctrines,
to chirp recklessly even in daytime, as if
a man had discovered the trace of truth
and wouldn't give it up.

而当冬天到来，大地一片沉寂，
我们如何管理我们的痛苦？
当薄薄的、蟋蟀的外壳，像一个
被无尽的歌唱掏空的命题，
我们如何处理我们卑贱的孤独？也许，

正是蟋蟀那易朽的弱点
在改变我们，以保证
这世界不被另外的答案掠取。所以，
你得把自己献给危险。你得知道，

一切都未结束，包括那歌声，
那内脏般的乐器：它的焦灼、恐惧，
和在其中失传的消息。

When winter comes, the earth grows still,
how do we manage our misery?
When the thinness of a cricket's carapace becomes
a proposition hollowed out by endless songs,
how do we handle our paltry loneliness? Perhaps,

it's the vulnerability of crickets
that changes us, ensures us that the world
won't be seized by a different answer. And so,
you must devote yourself to danger. You must know,

everything is not over yet, including that song,
that visceral instrument: the anxiety, the fear
and the message lost within.

卵石记

在水底,为阴影般的存在
创造出轮廓。恍如

自我的副本,对于
已逝,它是剩下的部分。无用的现状,
隐身谎言般寂静的内核,边缘
给探究的手以难以确定的
触摸感,偶尔

水落石出,它滚烫、干燥,像从一个
古老的部族中脱落出来。复又

沉入水底。在激流边
等待它出现像等待

时间失效。
看不见的深处,遗弃的废墟将它
置诸怀抱,却一直

Notes of a Pebble

At the bottom of the water, it creates an outline

for a shadowy existence. Like

a copy of oneself, the remainder

of what passed. Useless status quo,

a deceitful still core, the edge

gives a shifting sense

to an exploring hand, occasionally

the stone emerges from receding water, hot and dry,

as if set apart from an old tribe, then it

sinks into the bottom again. By the rapids,

you wait for it to reappear like

waiting for time to expire.

In the invisible depth, an abandoned ruin

embraces it

不知道该拿它怎么办。
——它就在那里,带着出生

之前的模样。静悄悄如同
因耽于幻想而不存在的事物。

but doesn't know what to do with it.

— It's there, in the shape it possessed

before birth, in the stillness, as if

too captivated by fantasy to exist.

面具

——只有面具留了下来,后面
已是永恒的虚空。
"以面具为界,时光分为两种:一种
认领万物;另一种,
和面具同在,无始无终。"

回声在周围沸腾,只有面具沉默。
现在,对面具的猜测,
是我们生活的主要内容。
有人拿起面具戴上,仿佛面具后面
一个空缺需要填补。而面具早已在
别的脸上找到自己的脸。面具后面那无法
破译的黑夜,谁出现在那里,
谁就会在瞬间瓦解。
——只有面具是结局,且从不怀念。

"面具的有效,在于它的面无表情。"
扣好面具的人,是提前来到
自己后世的人。那可怕的时刻,

Mask

— Only the mask is left,
behind it, an eternal void.
"Divided by the mask, there are two types of time:
one claims everything; another coexists
with the mask, without beginning or end."

Echoes seething on all sides, only the mask
remains still. So guessing about the mask
Becomes the main activity in our lives.
Someone puts on the mask, as if to fill a void
behind the mask, though the mask
has already found itself on another's face.
Behind the mask is the indecipherable night:
whoever appears there would collapse in an instant.
— The mask is the sole ending, and it never looks back.

"The mask is effective because it's expressionless."
The one who snaps on the mask arrives
early at his own future. At that terrible moment,

脑袋在，只是无法再摸到自己的脸。
——他曾匹马向前，狰狞面具
使恐惧出现在对手脸上……
当他归来，面具卸在一边，他的脸
仍需要表情的重新认领。
一种平静的忘却被留在远方。人，
这个深谙面具秘密的人，仿佛
着了魔，并听到了冥冥中传来的召唤。

"为何总是要重新开始？"如同
向另一个自我探询。说完，
他再次戴上面具，
出现在莫须有的描述中。

his head will be there, but he won't be able to touch his own face.

— He has been riding a horse, wearing a savage mask
putting horror on his opponent's face...
When he returns, takes off the mask,
needs to recuperate the emotion on his face.
He who understands the deep secret of a mask, as if
bewitched, hears the call from the hell.

"Why must we always begin again?"
He asked another self. Then
he puts on the mask again,
appears again in a groundless narration.

明月

通常我们认为,残月离去,
是为了把我们
生活中坏掉的东西拿走。

当它归来,穿过的仿佛不是里程,
而是来自
遥远岁月的那头。

一轮明月去过哪里?
没人知道。
有些夜晚,它泊在水中,
像靠着一个迷幻的港口。
有些时候,它泊在我们的听觉中,
自己带着岸。

我们知道它又一次变瘦的身影,
却难以说清,一代又一代,
它怎样和我们在一起?

Moon

We usually believe that the waning moon
departs to clean away
what is rotten in our lives.

When the moon returns, it
seems to have passed, not through distance,
but across a span of years.

Where has a bright moon ever been?
No one knows.
Some nights, it moors in the water
as if at a dreamy port.
Sometimes it parks in our hearing,
bringing its own shore.

Though knowing its shape that dwindles once more,
would we not wonder how it stays with us so long,
generation after generation?

城墙拆掉,游人散尽,
它把不为人知的部分轻轻
浮出水面。涟漪推动,一个
轻盈的怀抱若隐若现。

它再次出发,从一个图案
到一团光,进入天空
那敞开、无从感受的情感中。

The city wall is demolished, the tourists all gone.
In the water, the unknowable moon
floats gently. Ripples animate a lissome embrace,
only halfway visible.

It sets out, again, from a picture
to a halo of light. It enters the sky
into a wide-open, imperceptible emotion.

弹奏

有人在弹奏,
曲子里的人正在赶往人世。

弹奏,一遍又一遍,手指
摸到那些丢失的膝盖。

Playing Music

Someone is playing music;
within the melody, someone is rushing to the world.

Playing, over and over, fingers
are touching the knees no longer here.

宣纸

——事未休。
仍是这古老的造纸术:记忆,
沉在心跳危险的重构中。

——然则又是
一根竹管俯下身来,埋头苦干。
……憧憬、白日梦、耳鬓厮磨,再次
变成了陌生的地理学。

"墨,滞留在脱水、压平的地方……"
某个春风沉醉的晚上,我们
面壁而立,意识到:
一切都是熟稔的,只在留白里
仍有未被弄清的内容。

——而所有人都已不在场。
空气中浮动着
性的微尘,和纤维的雪。

Rice Paper

— Not yet done.
Ancient papermaking still goes on: memory is immersed
in a dangerous reconstruction of the heartbeat.

— Then again
a bamboo tube leans over, works hard.
...hope, daydream, hair and temples touching,
again, to become unfamiliar geography.

"Ink stays in the waterless, laid-out places..."
One night of intoxicating zephyrs, we
stood facing the wall, and realized
it may all be familiar, yet in the space left blank
there is content still undefined.

— And no one is present.
Floating in the air,
are dust-specks of sex and wisps of snow.

雨

雨来自比闪电更远的远方,
说着早已发生的事。
它的经历,它的再次经历……
万事变迁,但仍在雨的范畴中。

衣服挂在墙上,树冠在窗外猛烈摇晃……
万事变迁,我们的屋檐滴着水。
时间几乎征服了一切,除了雨,除了
雨再次从远方带来的东西。

Rain

Having come from farther than lightning, the rain told
a story that had already occurred.
What it experienced, and more afterwards...
Everything changed but is still within the sphere of rain.

Our clothes hanging on the wall, tree crown
   swaying wildly outside the window...
Everything changed, our eaves are dripping with water.
Time conquered almost everything except rain,
except for what was brought here, again, by the rain.

咖啡馆:忆旧

1

波纹在木柱里沉睡,
窗上的薄纱仿佛凉透了的花枝。

你沉静,过于温柔。
一阵风在我们心中旅行。
你的手停在幽暗的桌面上:一阵初雪
在季节里旅行。

2

拐过逼仄的楼梯,上面
就是初夏了。空气中,

浮动着类似记忆的暗影。
糖在咖啡里融化:某种不明的变化
在摸索时间的结构。

玻璃花瓶已经替代过什么。
一个下午
正消失于它的寂静。

In a Coffee Shop: Recalling the Past

1

Ripples sleep soundly in the wooden pillars,
gauze curtains are like flowers on a twig pierced by cold.

You are quiet, too gentle.
A gust of wind travels between our hearts.
Your hand rests on the darkened desk: fresh snow
travels in the seasons.

2

Turning from the tightly winding staircase, up above
is a day of early summer. In the air,

floats a shadow named memory.
Sugar dissolves in coffee: an indefinite change
gropes through the structure of the time.

A glass vase has taken something's place.
An afternoon
is vanishing in its silence.

阅读

读得如果太快,读者
就消失了。
让人苦恼的不是思想,也不是
厄运的裂变,而是
某种叙述口吻的耐心。

书立在书架上,像一截
被收藏的断壁。
——继续读吧,让风暴
从夹紧的书页间掉下来。或者,
先等一等,呆在
轰鸣之前那短暂的沉寂中。

天下大乱,这不重要,
重要的是,在一本刚刚合上的书里,
摧毁世界的风暴
回来了,
正守着忧心如焚的寂静。

Reading

If you read too fast, the reader in you
would vanish.
What torments us isn't thoughts, nor
the rupture of an ill fate, but the patience
in a narrative manner of speech.

Book stands on the shelf, like a piece
of broken wall kept in a collection.
— Let's keep reading, let the storm
slip out from pressed-together pages. Or,
let's wait a minute, stay
in the brief stillness before the roar.

Great chaos in the world, that's not important,
More important is that in a book just closed,
the destructive storm has come back,
to keep watch in the silence
that sears the brooding heart.

蜡烛

蜡烛亮了,守着
做梦的人,保证他不会从一个
被黑暗控制的地方醒来。

许多事已在梦中发生。有时,
蜡烛燃尽,人还没有醒。有时,
有人忘了把蜡烛点燃。
——它回到一件物品。

我见过甬道、地下室里的蜡烛,
那是在白天,它们像几个
正在整理旧档案的人:耐心地
捆好黑暗,把它们放在
一个被遗忘的世界中。

Candle

The candle is lit, keeping vigil over
a man in his dreams, ensuring that he will not
awaken in a place controlled by darkness.

In the dreams, many things have happened. Sometimes,
the candle burned out before the man woke up.
Sometimes, someone forgot to light the candle.
— It went back to being an object.

I have seen the candles during the day
in hallways and basements like
people organizing old files. They patiently
bundle the darkness, and store it
in a world we've forgotten.

峡谷记

峡谷空旷。谷底,
大大小小的石头,光滑,像一群
身体柔软的人在晒太阳。
它们看上去已很老了,但摸一摸,
皮肤又光滑如新鲜的孩童。
这是枯水季,时间慢。所有石头
都知道这个。石缝间,甚至长出了小草。时间,
像一片新芽在悄悄推送它多齿的叶缘;又像浆果内,
结构在发生不易察觉的裂变。
我在一面大石坡上坐下来,体会到
安全与危险之间那变化的坡度。脚下,
更多的圆石子堆在低处。沉默的一群,
守着彼此相似的历史。
而猛抬头,有座笔直的石峰,似乎已逃进天空深处。
在山谷中,虚无不可谈论,因为它又一次
在缓慢的疼痛中睡着了。
当危崖学会眺望,空空的山谷也一直在

Canyon

A vacant canyon, stones at the bottom,
big and small, smooth, like soft-skinned men
basking under the sun.
They look very old, but their skins, by touch,
are as smooth and fresh as children's.
In the arid season time is slow,
which all the stones know. Between cracks,
sprouts little grass blades. Time is like a sprout
quietly putting forth its multi-toothed leaves,
or a crack forming inside of a fruit, out of sight.
I sit down on a large stone slope, sensing
the steep increments between safety and danger.
More rounded stones pile up at my foot, a silent group,
sharing a similar history.
Quickly I look up, a towering peak seems to have fled
into the sky's depths.
In the canyon, we can't discuss the emptiness
because the slow pain has put it to sleep again.
As cliffs learn to overlook, a vacant canyon

学习倾听：呼啸的光阴只在

我们的身体里寻找道路。

那潜伏的空缺。那镂空之地送来的音乐。

has been learning to listen: only inside our bodies,

does the whizzing passage of time look for a path,

for a lurking vacancy, and the music from that vacancy.

蛇

爱冥想。
身体在时间中越拉越长。

也爱在我们的注意力之外
悄悄滑动,所以,
它没有脚,
不会在任何地方留下足迹。

当它盘成一团,像处在
一个静止的涟漪的中心。
那一圈一圈扩散的圆又像是
某种处理寂寞的方式。

蜕皮。把痛苦转变为
可供领悟的道理:一条挂在
树枝上晃来晃去的外套。又一次它从
旧我那里返回,抬起头

Snake

It loves to meditate.

Its body stretches longer and longer in time.

It also loves to shift quietly

beyond our attention, which is why

it has no feet,

leaves no footprints.

When it curls up, as if situated

at the still center of ripples,

from which circles expand outward

that is its way to deal with loneliness.

It sheds skin, turning pain into

comprehensible truth: an overcoat dangling

high on a branch. Once again it goes

the way of its old self, lifting its head

眺望远方……也就是眺望
我们膝盖以下的部分。
长长的信子,像火苗,但已摆脱了
感情的束缚。

偶尔,追随我们的音乐跳舞,
大多数时候不会
与我们交流。呆在
洞穴、水边,像安静的修士,

却又暴躁易怒。被冒犯的刹那
它认为:牙齿,
比所有语言都好用得多。

to look into the distance — looking
below our knees.
Its probing tongue is like a flame, but free from
emotional bondage.

It follows our music, occasionally, and dances
but most of the time it doesn't
associate with us. It stays in a cave, by the water,
like a silent monk,

yet it gets angry and irritable. If offended,
it believes only one doctrine: teeth
are superior in utility to all languages.

倾听

倾听一棵树,
每一阵风吹,它的声音都有
微妙的变化。所以,

质问简单的事物,如同扑打自身。
而爱一首简单的诗类似
听取绵绵不绝的回声。

——风穿过树林,
有时会传来咔嚓一声……
风穿过我们刚刚结束的谈话,带着
时间突然脱臼的声音。

Listening

Listen to a tree,
with each gust of wind, there are subtle changes
in sound, and so,

exploring simple things such as patting your own limbs
and loving a simple poem is like
listening to the endless echoes.

— Wind passes through the woods,
sometimes one hears a snapping sound ...
Wind passed through the talk we just finished, with
a sound of sudden dislocation in time.

初春

化石里的母兽抢夺水源,
它们用嗅觉和低低的吼声
教会一株忍冬走路。

——春天仍然是粗野的,
咒语,来自脏器里下沉的毒素。
干硬的龙爪槐沙沙响,在寻找
它丢失已久的动物性。

残雪抗衡催眠,死亡如水银,
泥泞在替旅人创造命运。
一缕长途跋涉的光在被浪费之前,
做成我手中这支玫瑰。

Early Spring Day

A fossilized she-beast seizes the water source.
By smell and low roar,
it teaches a honeysuckle tree to walk.

— Spring is still rough and wild,
its spell is cast by toxins settling in the viscera.
The claw-limbed pagoda tree rustles, groping
for its long-lost animality.

Residual snow resists hypnosis, death like quicksilver,
soupy mire decides the fate of travelers.
A light ray from afar, before being wasted,
becomes a rose in my hand.

天文学

如果群星被万有引力控制在
各自的轨道。万幸,
还有些小星星是自由的。
——它们在隐秘中穿过黑暗,并在
靠近我们时成为闪亮的流星。

必有神力庇护了这微小的自由;
必有某种爱,任性,不怕毁灭。
必有人在更遥远的地方,为火和黑子
各写下一首赞美诗。

必有人爱得像超导体……
必有伤害,像彗尾,像量子纠缠,
必有人精通第六感,在膨胀中发现了
心中自有主张的宇宙。
必有激情的磁场娴熟于吞噬,并在
对迷信和愚昧的继承中

Astronomy

If all celestial bodies are held by gravity
in their tracks, and if, by pure luck, some
of the small ones are free
— passing through the darkness in secret
and becoming bright meteors when near us.

There must be a divine power to succor this tiny freedom,
There must be love, willfulness, no fear of destruction.
There must be one who stays in a farther place,
    for the sake of both a flame and a black spot,
writing a praise poem.

There must be one whose love is like a superconductor...
There must be hurt, like a comet tail,
like quantum entanglement,
There must be one with a strong sixth sense who,
amid the expansion, discovers a self-guiding universe.
There must be a passionate magnetic field, well-versed
    in engulfment,
which accepts the black hole that belongs
to the superstition and ignorance it will inherit.

接受了黑洞。我们赞过的神，
闹过的鬼，都在其中消失。因此，

当一个遥远的星系消失，必有心脏
无声落入水面。而望远镜前，
有人紧紧相拥，并感受到了对方体内
那起伏的悲戚。因此，

爱是新生，也是一种特殊的死法，
幸存者会变成新的元素，或暗物质，
看不见，但能被感觉到，并需要
在无人相爱的空虚中费力地
继续证明其存在。

The gods we praised, the ghosts we were haunted by
are evaporating in it. So,

when a distant galaxy disappears, there must be a heart
quietly falling into water. And in front of the telescope,
there are people embracing, feeling the ebb and flow
of sorrow in each other's body. So,

love is a new life and a particular way to die.
Survivors will become new elements, or dark matter,
unseen but capable of being felt. In the void
where there is no mutual love, they need to try hard
to prove its existence.

果园

幸福过于猛烈时,像复仇……
黑暗中,一只苹果
突然离开枝头。
"昨夜,谁的心紧跳,追随声音而去?"
雨水太多,众人昏睡,
阴影,携带着蓄积已久的重量
从大地上一滑而过。

——夏日果园,闪烁的光斑
曾试图控制所有时间。
在树下,我侧耳倾听,
洁净果肉里,小溪在冲刷。
幸福之事,在体会中,总是慢的。

树枝伸展,绿浪掩卷,
彼时,苍老的果农告诉我:
苹果之死,万事休,犹如人从梦中遁去。

Orchard

Overly strong happiness is like an act of revenge...
In the dark, an apple
suddenly left the branch.
"Last night, whose heartbeat went pursuing the voice?"
Too much a rain makes people drowsy,
Its shadow, carrying long-accumulated weight
slides over the earth.

— Summer orchard, light spots flickering,
once tried to seize every bit of time.
Under the tree, I listen carefully,
to a stream rushing in untainted fruit pulp,
happiness is always slow to be experienced.

Tree branches stretching, green waves swirling;
once, an old fruit farmer told me:
In an apple's death, everything ends,
like when a person flees from his own dream.

当归

种当归的人,背影
像干裂尘沙。
他蹲在田埂上抽烟,长久地
守着幼小秧苗。
当归长成,是多年后的事。

三轮车在小镇上突突响,有人
在梦里翻土。
而真正的生活是一阵低语;是泥土
守着的腥甜阴影。
——黑暗深处,我们慢慢活着,
依靠彼此的躯体把死亡忘却。

太多的风在制药厂上空盘旋。正是这
无始终的呼唤一年年
把当归变成了沉默之物。

注:＊当归,中药材名。

Angelica

A man planting angelica, the shape of his back
shows like dry, cracked sand.
He squats at the field's edge, smoking, for a long time
Watching over young seedlings.
It takes many years for angelica to grow up.

A three-wheeler runs noisily in town, someone
is plowing the field in a dream,
but real life is conducted in whispers; it is soil
keeping close to a musty, sweet shadow.
— deep in the dark, we live slowly,
relying on each other's body to forget death.

Hovering over the pharmaceutical plant, there is too much wind.
Endless summoning calls, year after year,
made angelica into a silent thing.

* Angelica is a kind of Chinese herbal medicine.

初秋书

长廊在呼吸,群鸟飞掠;
树枝晃动,风在把握,

江湖已远,
我去拜访一个更深的年代。那里,
还俗的僧人是个好木匠。
桌子上,不倒翁在发呆。

——诗该怎样写出?也许
发生过的一切都是真的。
此间,藤花开,小狮子在山墙上玩耍。
而高速路上,有人
正加大油门,逼迫地平线把尚未
消化掉的远方吐了出来。

The Book of Early Autumn

Breaths are drawn on the verandah, birds swoop by,
Branches swaying, wind gripping.

The waterfront is far away;
I visit an even further era, where an ex-monk
is an excellent carpenter; on a table
a round-bottomed doll dozes off.

— How to write a poem? Perhaps
whatever happened is the truth.
Here at this moment, on the wall, vines
are blooming, lion cubs playing.
On the highway, someone
is stepping hard on the gasoline, forcing the horizon
to spit out undigested places in the distance.

深夜的十字路口

深夜,十字路口变成了十字架,
沉浸黑暗中。

偶尔有人从那里经过,
像天国里的最后一个人。

Late Night at the Crossroad

Late at night, the crossroads becomes a cross
immersed in the darkness.

Occasionally someone passes,
like the last person in heaven.

蝶

回声适合折叠成花纹。
一个尖音,
适合刺在一阵风逃离的背上。
落向灌木和桥头的,不像翅膀,
更像一种秘密的语调。

花都开了,风也
重新开始了。我们案头的书信,仍是一个
以沉默制造的斑斓迷宫。

而当它继续飞,帮一节光
取回它的脊椎;帮一个
纹身男子来到春天的城外:在所有

翩然而过的族类中,
它最飘乎,最适合捕捉
气候的变化,和你我心中那闪烁、
难以把握的瞬间。

BUTTERFLY

The echo is suitable to be folded into a pattern.
A sharp sound, suitable
to be tattooed on the back of a fleeing wind.
Dropping onto shrubs and bridge abutments, more like
the intonation of baffling speech than like wings.

Flowers are all blooming, and the wind
has begun again. The letters on our desk
are still a motley maze made by the silence.

As th·e butterfly is flying, restoring the backbone
to a segment of light, sending a tattooed man
out of the city in spring: amid

all the species that have whisked by,
the butterfly is the most capricious, yet the most eligible
to capture a change in climate or the flickering,
elusive moment in our hearts.

夏花

南风送来的爱人,
影子看上去有点甜。
我骑着自行车,带她去见我的母亲。
一路上,她每讲一句话,体重
就减轻一点。
她去小解,从一大蓬绿植
后面回来,她是快乐的。
地米开罢,金佛莲
正在开,一粒粒花骨朵,像控制着
声音的纽扣,带着夏的神秘,
和微微羞怯。

Summer Flower

The south wind sent over my lover,

with her sweet-looking shadow.

I rode a bicycle, taking her to see my mother.

Along the way, every time she spoke,

her weight diminished.

She went to pee and came back

from behind an awning of plants. She was happy.

After the rice plants flowered, one by one

the golden Buddha lotuses started blooming,

from buds like sound-control buttons, imbued with

mystery of summer and a touch of shyness.

私生子

有人走了,我们身边,
空出一个位子。

大卡车从街上隆隆驶过,
我们身边空出一个位子。
它在震动,它的虚空暴露了出来。

后来,有人坐在那里,
背影里拖着一条长长的马路。
而那消失的人,在另外的地方,
代表我们活着。

最后,当我们全都
已不在现场,有人看见,
一辆卡车从那座位上起身离去,
带走了马路,
留下了椅子隐秘的身世。

Illegitimate Child

Someone went away; the place beside us
is left empty.

A big truck is rumbling down the street,
the place beside us is left empty,
shaking, its emptiness exposed.

Later, someone comes to sit there.
Past his figure seen from behind, a road stretches.
As for the vanished one, in another place
he lives for us.

At last when we are all
out of the scene, someone sees a truck
getting up from that seat and leaving too,
taking away the road
leaving the chair's concealed particulars.

登天

无数尖峰,正在通往天空的路上。
亿万年了,它们干得不错。

我也在登天,
当我大汗淋漓出现在峰顶,
也成了一个云彩上的人。

天空中有什么?
我和山都仰着脸。大地上
峰海起伏。没有一处虚空让我们
如此痴迷。虽然,
那最高的一盏并不比
最矮的一个知道的更多。

我下山来,回首间,
山又长高了一截。
有人还在攀登,他将到达

Up to The Sky

Countless peaks, on the way to the sky.
Hundreds of millions of years, they've done an excellent job.

I too am on the way to the sky,
when I appear on the peak, sweating profusely,
I too am above the clouds.

What is in the sky?
Mountain and I are looking up. On the earth,
a sea of peaks undulates. No void could make us
so obsessed. Even so,
the highest peak knows no better than
the shortest one.

I come down the mountain, looking back,
it has grown taller.
Someone is still climbing and will arrive

我没到过的地方。
也许有一天,一个从更高处下来的人,
会把答案带回人间。

at the place that I had never been.

Perhaps the one from a higher place, one day,

will bring the answer down to our world.

传说

神话发蓝。勇士无法分类。
大海的悲伤使书页悸动,
不经意的道别已变成永别。

下午三点,一阵细雨,
木马成灰。埃及人建造金字塔。
雨停了,阿基米德
在沙上划出又一道难题。

Legend

Myths look blue, warriors unclassifiable.
Book pages disturbed by sorrow of the sea.
An unintended goodbye becomes a farewell.

Three o'clock in the afternoon, in drizzling rain,
wooden horse turns to dust. Egyptians build the pyramids.
The rain stops. Archimedes
draws another puzzle on the sand.

称体重

称体重时,看见
指针忽然猛烈颤动了几下,指向
我体重之外的某个地方……

然后它退回,
假装从没触碰过那里。

Weighing Myself

As I weighed myself, I saw
the needle twitching drastically a few times,
pointing to the place beyond my weight...

then it moved back,
pretending that I've never been there.

箭毒蛙

他用一根针刺死它,
取它的毒液。它只有
几厘米大,但他知道
只需几滴,杀死一只巨兽就足够了。
还有一次,他把它活着
放到火上烤。
火很小,它在火上痉挛,死得慢。
雨林摇晃,但他的手
很稳,把毒液稳稳地
涂在箭头上。然后他静静地
看着它蹬腿,皮肤
冒泡,嘴
偶尔张一下,如同目睹一颗小心脏
在某人的胸腔里提前
停止了跳动。

Piercing a Poisonous Frog

He stabbed it with a needle

to extract the venom. It was only centimeters long,

but few drops could kill a huge beast.

Another time, he cooked a frog alive,

 a flame was low, it twitched and died slowly.

The jungle was tossing, but his hands were

steady enough to paint venom

on the arrow. Then he quietly

watched its legs kicking, skin

sizzling, mouth

opening a few times, like a tiny heart

stopping prematurely in someone's chest.

致谢词

本集中的某些作品曾在《十三片叶子：中国当代优秀诗人选集》（谢炯、白金沙合作翻译，2018年美国猫头鹰出版社）中出版。另外，感谢梅丹理先生对本集修改和编辑做出的巨大贡献。

Acknowledgement

Some poems in this book appeared previously in Thirteen Leaves: Selected Poems of Contemporary Chinese Poets (co-translated by Joan Xie and Sam Perkins, published by Three Owls Press, USA in 2018). I also offer my heartfelt thanks to Mr. Denis Mair who offered editorial contributions to this book.

图书在版编目（CIP）数据

石雕与蝴蝶：胡弦诗选：汉、英／胡弦著；谢炯译.
-- 北京：中国青年出版社，2020.1
ISBN 978-7-5153-5732-4

Ⅰ.①石… Ⅱ.①胡…②谢… Ⅲ.①诗集－中国－当代－汉、英 Ⅳ.①I227

中国版本图书馆CIP数据核字(2019)第292078号

策划出品：小众书坊
责任编辑：彭明榜 + 吕达
书籍设计：孙初 + 文小婧

中国青年出版社 出版 发行
社址：北京东四12条21号
小众书坊地址：北京东城区后圆恩寺胡同甲1号
电话：(010) 64011190
网上销售：京东商城小众雅集图书专营店
北京精彩世纪印刷科技有限公司印刷　新华书店经销

889mm×1194mm 1／32 7.75印张 113千字
2020年2月北京第1版 2020年2月北京第1次印刷
定价：50.00元